Angela Thirkell

Angela Thirkell, granddaughter of Edward Burne-Jones, was born in London in 1890. At the age of twenty-eight she moved to Melbourne, Australia where she became involved in broadcasting and was a frequent contributor to the British periodicals. Mrs. Thirkell did not begin writing novels until her return to Britain in 1930; then, for the rest of her life, she produced a new book almost every year. Her stylish prose and deft portrayal of the human comedy in the imaginary county of Barsetshire have amused readers for decades. She died in 1961, just before her seventy-first birthday.

Mrs. Thirkell writes with an asperity and wit and gracious clowning that are all her own.

—San Francisco Chronicle

Where Trollope would have been content to arouse a chuckle, [Angela Thirkell] is constantly provoking us to hilarious laughter. . . . To read her is to get the feeling of knowing these Barsetshire folk as well as if one had been born and bred in the County.

—Kirkus Reviews

There's just no stopping after one novel.

—Publishers Weekly

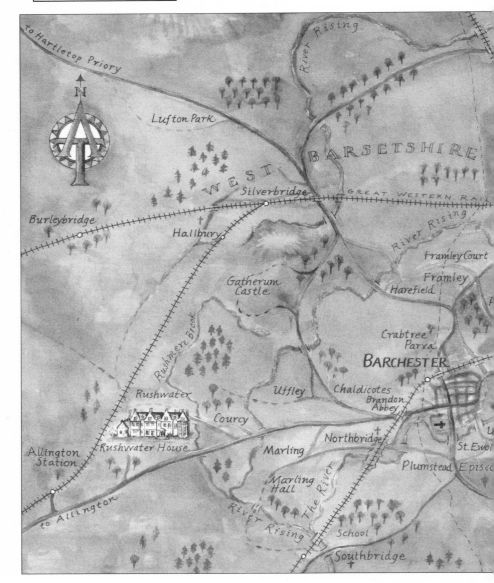

Table of Explanation

Roads...............	
Railways...........	++++++++++
Rivers...............	～～
Towns..............	HOGGLESTOCK
Parish Villages...	Puddingdale
Small Villages....	Little Misfit
Mansions...........	*Pomfret Towers*

0   1   2   3   4   5

Scale of Miles

to Hartletop Priory

N

River Rising

Lufton Park

BARSETSHIRE

WEST

Silverbridge

GREAT WESTERN RAIL

Burleybridge

Hallbury

River Rising

Framley Court

Framley

Gatherum Castle

Harefield

Rushmere Brook

Crabtree Parva

BARCHESTER

Rushwater

Uffley

Chaldicotes

Brandon Abbey

Courcy

St. Ewol

Allington Station

Rushwater House

Marling

Northbridge

Plumstead Episco

to Allington

Marling Hall

The River

River Rising

School

Southbridge

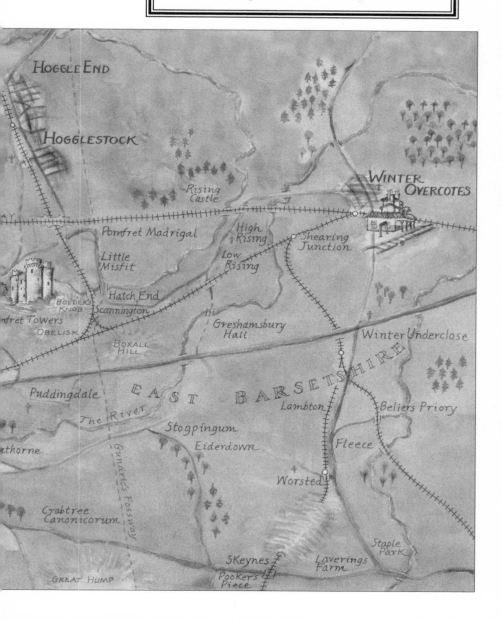

A Map of the County of

BARSETSHIRE

Showing the Situations of the various great Estates and Seats

HOGGLE END

HOGGLESTOCK

Rising Castle

WINTER OVERCOTES

Pomfret Madrigal

High Rising

Shearing Junction

Little Misfit

Low Rising

BOLDERS KNOB

Hatch End

Scannington

fret Towers

OBELISK

Greshamsbury Hall

Winter Underclose

BOXALL HILL

Puddingdale

EAST BARSETSHIRE

The River

Lambton

Beliers Priory

athorne

Stogpingum

Fleece

Eiderdown

Gundric's Fossway

Worsted

Crabtree Canonicorum

Staple Park

GREAT HUMP

Skeynes

Laverings Farm

Pooker's Piece

THE
DEMON
IN THE
HOUSE

A Novel by
Angela Thirkell

 MOYER BELL

Kingston, Rhode Island & Lancaster, England

Published by Moyer Bell
This Edition 2006
Copyright © 1934 by the Executors of
Angela Thirkell

LIBRARY OF CONGRESS
CATALOGING-IN-PUBLICATION DATA

Thirkell, Angela Mackail, 1890-1961.
The demon in the house

192 p.   21.5 cm.
1. Mothers and sons—England—Fiction.
2. Boys—England—Fiction 3. Country life—Fiction.
4 England—Fiction
I. Title.
PR6039.H43D4   2006
823'.912-dc20   96-45999
ISBN 1-55921-159-8   CIP

Cover Illustration: Albert Besnard, A Family, 1890

Printed in the United States of America.

Distributed in North America by
Moyer Bell, 549 Old North Road, Kingston, Rhode Island 02881,
401–783–5480, www.moyerbellbooks.com
and in the United Kingdom, Eire, and Europe by
Gazelle Book Services Ltd., White Cross Mills, High Town,
Lancaster LA1 1RN England,
1–44–1524–68765, www.gazellebooks.co.uk

THE
DEMON
IN THE
HOUSE

LIST OF CONTENTS

1

EASTER HOLIDAYS

CHAPTER **I**

THE BICYCLE

When Tony Morland wasn't at school he lived with his mother in the country. His father had died so long ago that he couldn't remember him, so he just thought that fathers were things other people had. As his three elder brothers were usually abroad or at sea, he missed the fraternal snubbing which is supposed to improve the character. His mother sometimes tried to be a little unkind to him, because she felt the responsibility of being a father and mother rolled into one, but she wasn't very successful. Mothers, as far as Tony could see, were just things that everybody had. One put up with them as one put up with cricket, M. Dubois the French master, Mr. Prothero, who gave one impositions just for doing nothing at all, like pushing another chap at drill and drawing pictures on one's Ovid, or as one put up with anything else that had obviously been there for ever and would go on for ever. Also he liked his mother very much, and sometimes hugged her to strangulation point, till she had to beg for mercy.

His mother wrote books to earn enough money to have a house in the country and send Tony to school. Tony had read some of her books, but did not think very highly of them. They all had a good deal of what he called Love Trash in them, a subject which his favorite authors scorned. But luckily Laura Morland didn't in the least mind what Tony thought of her books, nor what any one else thought, so long as she could please the people who get books from the libraries. And luckily for Tony, the library people liked his mother's books much better than he did.

Tony was rather an important person, as it was his last year before going on to the upper school, and he had trousers instead of knickerbockers in term time, and was a monitor.

"Being a monitor gives you great power," he said to his mother while she was unpacking his trunk on the first day of the Easter holidays. "The little chaps are afraid to cheek you, and matron doesn't mind if you bring hair fixative to school."

"But I do mind if you bring it home," said his mother, "especially if you don't put the stopper in properly and it comes out all over your clothes. Look."

She held up a white flannel shirt liberally stained with Butygloss Hair Fixative.

"I know," said Tony. "Mother, can I have a bicycle these holidays?"

"We might hire one, but I'm not going to buy you one till your legs are longer. You know you still can't manage a man's size, even with the saddle put right down."

"But two of the chaps have small size bikes, mother."

"I dare say they have, Tony, but I can't afford to get you a bicycle that you'll grow out of in a year or two. Stretch your legs out a bit, and then I'll think about it. We'll go down to the village in a day or two and see what we can do."

The village, at one end of which Mrs. Morland lived, was called High Rising. Tony's special friends there were Mr. Mallow, the stationmaster, Sid Brown, the porter, and his brother, Mr. Brown, owner of the garage, Dr. Ford, Dr. Ford's housekeeper, Mrs. Mallow, who was also the stationmaster's aunt, and the two younger Vicarage girls, Rose and Dora. The chief quality which Tony required in his friends was an infinite capacity to listen to what he said. Most of his intimate circle were ready to be an admiring audience, but Dr. Ford and Dora Gould were unhappy exceptions. Dr. Ford either took no notice of what Tony said or told him to shut up, but he was a decent chap who would take one in his car if he happened to be going anywhere in the direction of where the hounds were meeting, or let one do chemistry in his little laboratory in the garden.

As for Dora Gould, though she had her uses she was undoubtedly a cheeky kid. Rose Gould, who was fourteen and a year older than Tony, admired him deeply and was content to sit watching him for hours while he laid out railway systems in his mother's garden and talked aloud to himself about the electric engine he was going to buy when he had saved up enough pocket money. But Dora, who was twelve and a year younger than Tony, showed a lamentable want of interest in railways and talked a great deal about an imaginary country called Dorland, after herself, its population, industries, and chief physical features. In self-defense Tony had been obliged to create a country of his own, which he called Morland. He broke the news of this country to Rose and Dora when they were all upstairs in Tony's playroom one day.

"You're copying me," said Dora indignantly, on hearing of Morland.

"I'm not. Morland is a real name; and as a matter of fact it was called after us hundreds of years ago. Dorland is just a silly make-up name. How high is the highest mountain in Dorland?"

"How high is the highest in Morland?" asked Dora cautiously.

"Six miles."

"Well, the highest mountain in Dorland is six and a half miles high."

"I know," said Tony, "but that's counting from sea level. I count mine from where it rises from a very high plateau in the middle of the island, so really it is seven miles high. Mother is going to get me a bike these hols."

"Oh, Tony," said Rose, "one of your own?"

"Well, practically, because she is going to hire it. You'll see me scorching through the village at about twenty-five. Twenty-five m.p.h.," he added, seeing Rose's look of perplexity. "Oh, well, if you can't understand anything, twenty-five miles an hour."

Dora's face of admiration and subsequent, though temporary,

silence were tributes to Tony's powers of boasting. Rose, who had been mildly jealous of her younger sister's inventive powers, cringed openly before Tony.

"May I come into Morland, Tony?" she asked humbly. "Dora won't have me in Dorland."

"By all means," said Tony graciously. "I'll give you a bit of land for yourself called Rosebush."

"Oh, thank you, Tony, what a lovely name."

"I know. It's really a place in Pembrokeshire. You get there by the South Wales Express as far as Carmarthen, and then you take a rail motor. Do you know what a rail motor is?"

"No."

"Well, you wouldn't understand if I explained. The South Wales Express is a stupid name, because it is only express as far as Cardiff, and then it stops everywhere and takes hours. But all the same, the Great Western is the best railway in England. If I had a lot of money I'd buy it, and run aluminum stream-line engines like the new American ones. I'd break all the records. And I'd have air-conditioned coaches."

"What are they like?" asked Rose.

"Coaches that are air-conditioned, of course."

"All the Dorland coaches are like that," said Dora, recovering her poise.

"I know," said Tony. "But they can't be because it's a new invention and all the new inventions get to Morland first, and Dorland is years behind. Would you like a snack?"

Rose and Dora said they would.

"All right," said Tony, "I'll go down and get something, and you can let the train go around the lines while I'm away, but don't alter the points or put the engine into reverse."

Tony leapt and clattered downstairs and into the kitchen, where Stoker, Mrs. Morland's very fat middle-aged maid, was making pastry. Stoker had been with Mrs. Morland for a great many years, and though she was fond of Tony's three elder brothers, who were now grown-up and scattered about the world, her chief devotion was for Tony. For him she made special puddings, substituted fried potatoes for boiled, took up breakfast on a tray if he was late, listened endlessly to his talk, and imparted to him the folklore of Plaistow, her unromantic eastern birthplace.

"Well, Master Tony," she said, "how's the railway this morning?"

"It's all right. Oh, Stokes, could I have some snacks for me and the girls? They are frightfully hungry."

"I dare say they are," said Stoker, who lived in permanent feud with the Vicarage cook. "There's many a morning when those poor young ladies can't eat what's set before them, I'll be bound. What do you want. Bread and dripping?"

"Oh, good for you, Stokes."

Stoker heaved herself up and fetched from the larder a bowl of excellent beef dripping with those rich, dark patches in it, so dear to the connoisseur. While she was spreading it thickly on three large slices of bread Tony sat on the table and ate the odds and ends of uncooked pastry that lay about.

"I'm going to have a bike these hols, Stokes," he announced.

"First I've heard of it," said Stoker, showering pepper and salt onto the dripping. "Who's going to keep it clean?"

"I am, of course."

"So you say," remarked Stoker without heat.

"That's wrong, Stokes. You ought to say 'Sez you.'"

"Say what you like, Master Tony, I know what bikes are. Just like rabbits and canaries. It all means more work for your poor mother and me. Take your dripping up to the young ladies and don't eat any more of that pastry, it might swell in your inside. I had a cousin carried off that way."

"Where did they carry him?" asked Tony, getting off the table.

"London hospital. And what they done to him no one knows, nor ever will, but his wife never set eyes on him alive again."

"Did they kill him then?" asked Tony, with shining eyes.

"No, it was her got killed. Knocked down by a motor car the day he come out of hospital. She had a lovely voice and used to sing like a lark. Get along now, Master Tony, or I'll never get on with lunch."

The bread and dripping was gratefully received, and Tony added a new town called Drippingham to his country in its honor.

After lunch his mother told him to come to the village with her.

"Oh, mother, need I? I had something frightfully important to do."

"No need if you don't want a bicycle," said his mother coldly.

"Oh, good for you, mother. Let's go to Mr. Brown. He might have one at the garage."

Accordingly Mrs. Morland and Tony set out for the garage. Mr. Brown unfortunately had only a full-sized man's bicycle in stock, and though the saddle was lowered as far as possible, Tony's legs did not reach the lowest point of the pedals. Mr. Brown offered a lady's bicycle, but Tony's despair at the idea of this humiliation was so deep that his mother weakly consented to search elsewhere.

"You see, mother, I couldn't possibly ride a girl's bike," he explained as they walked towards the general store where Mr. Reid occasionally had an odd bicycle. "They aren't strong enough, and I couldn't get up speed properly. Besides, what would people think if they saw me on a girl's bike?"

"I shouldn't think they would take any notice at all."

"Oh, mother, they would. All the kids would laugh at me if they saw me on a girl's bike."

Mr. Reid had just let his own bicycle out to a visitor for the whole of the Easter holidays, but suggested that Sid Brown, the porter at the station, might be willing to hire his out for a week or two. As Sid Brown was a little man, Mrs. Morland thought it worth trying, so she and Tony walked on to the station.

"Mother," said Tony, "you know Morland?"

"Your country do you mean?" asked Laura.

"Of course. Well, I've got a new town there now, called Dripping-ham. It's because old Stokes gave us a snack of bread and dripping, to me and Rose and Dora. You see, Drippingham because of dripping. Isn't it a good name? The ham part doesn't mean ham of course, but just the sort of ham that you get in real names."

"Like East Ham?" said his mother.

"Yes. Don't you think it's an awfully good name? And I let Rose have a bit of my country and call it Rosebush. There is really a station called Rosebush and you can only get there by a rail motor. Mother, why don't we have a rail motor on our line? I'd love to see a rail motor. I'd like to drive one, and I'd simply whiz up and down the line. How do you think rail motors are worked, mother?"

"I don't know. Come along, Tony, and don't gabble so much, and we can see the down train go through."

When the down express had successfully torn on its way through the station Mrs. Morland approached Sid Brown, who said he didn't rightly think he could spare his bike, but his cousin Henry had a racing bike, and as he had broke his ankle and wouldn't be about for a bit, perhaps he would consider letting the younger gentleman have it. Tony's eyes glowed at the thought of a racing bicycle, and he implored his mother to hire it at once. Sid's cousin Henry lived a mile or so away, near Low Rising, so the Morlands set off on their journey again. Owing to his broken ankle Henry Brown was at home and quite willing to let Tony have the bicycle if he could ride it. The saddle was lowered. Tony fell off three times and declared it a perfect fit. An arrangement was then made by which Sid's cousin Henry was to have five shillings a week for the use of his bicycle, and Tony was to keep it clean and restore it in good condition.

"Can I ride it home now, mother?" said Tony.

"I suppose so," said his mother with resignation. "But do for goodness' sake be careful with motors."

Tony mounted his steed and dashed off down the road towards High Rising, wobbling violently as he went. He rapidly disappeared around a bend in the road and his mother walked on after him, telling herself that she really must remember that boys were not brought home dead on a shutter simply because they rode bicycles.

When Tony had begun his bicycling career she had tried to take up bicycling again herself, so that she might accompany him, and at least be in at his death, but the plan was not a success. Laura Morland, who had hardly bicycled since motors became common, was extremely frightened. Any expedition that included a main road was agony to her, as she pedaled desperately away, hugging the edge of the road, her teeth painfully clenched, her hands on both brakes, terrified of death before and behind her. Tony's methods were not helpful to her. He either scorched past her at reckless speed or rode at a snail's pace, frequently turning around in the road. When he was speeding his unhappy mother could not keep up with him. If he went slowly she had to ride on ahead, sending despairing glances backwards from time to time to see if he had been run down by a motor-coach while performing his evolutions.

After a terrible day on which Tony had ridden, like John Gilpin, into the country far away, while his mother sat and cried with mingled rage and fear halfway up a steep hill, Laura had renounced bicycling for ever and given her bicycle to one of Rose and Dora's elder sisters. For the future, she decided, it would be better to wait at home for the news of Tony's death or mutilation than to be left crying by the roadside.

By this time Laura had reached the bend of the road, but there was no sign of Tony in the half mile of straight road which lay between her and High Rising. The well-known agonizing symptoms of anxiety began to make themselves felt. Instinctively she walked a little faster, as if by hurrying she could overtake whatever evil fate was threatening her youngest son. A car approached from the village. As it came within hailing distance it slowed down, and Dr. Ford waved from the driving seat.

"Have you seen Tony?" she shouted.

Dr. Ford put on the brakes violently. His car put all its four feet together, slithered, and came to a standstill.

"What?" shouted Dr. Ford, getting into reverse.

"Have you seen Tony anywhere, or a bicycle?" she repeated, feeling thoroughly ashamed, but unable to restrain herself.

"Not yet," said Dr. Ford. "If I pass him I'll tell him to hurry up," with which kind though uncomprehending remark he sped away towards Low Rising.

Mrs. Morland plodded feverishly on, her throat beginning to feel thick and choked with hasty walking and suppressed tears. She had a burning desire to be very angry with someone, but no one was at hand.

"Men are all selfish," she said aloud, lumping Dr. Ford and Tony together in this sweeping statement.

A bicycle bell behind her made her start and dash to the side of the road. A bicycle flashed past her, and to her relief and fury she saw Tony, well bent down over the racing handles, his feet going madly. Before she could recover her voice he had slowed down, turned, and was by her side.

"You didn't expect me, mother, did you?" he asked proudly.

"I didn't."

"I knew you wouldn't. I went on like mad as far as the Vicarage and simply whizzed down the lane and along the field path and got back into the road. I saw Dr. Ford. What do you think Dr. Ford thought when he saw me on the bicycle, mother?"

"I don't know."

"I expect he thought I looked like a real racing bicyclist. Mother, did you know that racing bicycles don't have free wheels? They have fixed wheels. Why do you think they have fixed wheels, mother?"

"Perhaps it's easier to race with a fixed wheel," said Mrs. Morland, in whom relief had now got the upper hand of anger.

"Yes, I know. But it's jolly hard work, I can tell you, to keep one's feet going. I had to pedal away like anything going down the Vicarage Lane. I expect Rose and Dora would be very interested to see me pedaling away so quickly, wouldn't they? Mother, can I stop at the Vicarage and show them the bicycle?"

"All right, but be back for tea."

"Oh, mother, need I?"

"Well, you must be back by six. If you aren't I shall disgrace you by coming to fetch you," said Mrs. Morland. Tony was riding around and around her as she walked, and the effect of addressing him at all points of the compass was making her feel a little giddy.

"Good on you, mother," said Tony cheerfully, and rode off.

When Laura got home she had some tea and felt more composed. Tony could not come to any harm at the Vicarage, so she could write letters or read in peace till six o'clock. Accordingly she sat down at her desk, but even as she wrote to Tony's headmaster about a scholarship exam which Tony was to sit for—though more as a gesture than with any hope of getting him through—a horrid thought intruded itself. Supposing Tony had not gone to the Vicarage. Supposing he had gone off on his own. No one would know where he was. His corpse would probably not be found till the following morning. Just as she was telling herself that she must *not* ring up Mrs. Gould and enquire if Tony was with Rose and Dora, Stoker came in to clear away the tea-things.

"Shall I leave something out for Master Tony?" asked Stoker.

"No, Stoker, he has gone to the Vicarage to show his bicycle to the little girls. We managed to get one from Sid Brown's cousin Henry. He has broken his ankle and can't get about at present."

"I used to do a bit of biking myself," said Stoker.

"Did you, Stoker?"

"When I was a girl I did. Around the Victoria Park, you've no idea. Daisy they used to call me at home, out of the song, you know—'A Bicycle Made For Two.' I'd need a bicycle made for two to carry me nowadays," said Stoker with a music-hall wink. "Tricycle's more my style. Always try a tricycle before you buy a bicycle, as the saying is. Well, I'll do an extra lot of pancakes for tonight. Master Tony will need something after tea at the Vicarage. Grocer's cake as likely as not."

"Oh, Stoker," said her mistress as she was leaving the room with the tray, "would you ring up the Vicarage and ask Mrs. Gould to see that Tony leaves at six sharp?"

Stoker put her tray down with a bang on a chest in the hall.

"Now, don't you commence to worry," she said, with hearty scorn for Mrs. Morland's anxiety. "Master Tony won't come to no harm, bike or no bike, and there's no call for you to waste money 'phoning up the Vicarage."

Laura meekly accepted Stoker's advice, and was rewarded by the return of her youngest son at a quarter to six, bursting with information.

"Mother," he began, "we had a splendid time. I simply whizzed up and down the lane for the girls to see, and after tea I showed them how slowly I can ride and how to turn in the narrow part of the lane, and they thought it was jolly good. I told them I was going to be a professional and do dirt track racing. Dora wants to have a dirt track in Dorland, but I told her she couldn't because they aren't invented in Dorland yet. I shall have a splendid one in Morland, about ten miles around, and I'll go whizzing around it. What's the fastest a racing bike can go, do you think, Mother?"

"I haven't the faintest idea."

"But about how fast should you *think?*"

"I don't know. As much as twenty miles an hour?"

"Oh, mother!"

"Well, fifteen then."

"Oh, mother! Fifteen! Mother, I bet you I could do forty, easily, on a good dirt track with a motor bike in front of me. Mother, wouldn't it be splendid if we could have a dirt track in the garden?"

"You look like a dirt track yourself," said his mother dispassionately. "What on earth have you got on your hands and jersey?"

Tony's blue eyes shone with innocence.

"On my jersey, mother? Oh, that's only oil. I was showing Rose and Dora how to oil the bike. It will be useful for them when they have bikes of their own. One ought to keep one's bike well oiled, you know," he added virtuously.

Mrs. Morland drew her son nearer to her and examined his jersey. It and his hands were liberally smeared with a thick green mixture which she recognized as motor grease.

"But you don't oil bicycles with motor oil," she said.

"I know. But we hadn't any bike oil, so Dora gave me some of her father's lubricating oil out of the garage. I thought you'd like me to keep the bike oiled, mother, considering we've got to let Henry have it back in good condition. It's running splendidly now, mother. Come and look."

Tony led the way to the back yard, where the bicycle stood propped against a wall. Every part of it which could conceivably be thought to require oil was plastered with lubricant. Tony wheeled it around to let his mother see his handiwork.

"I'll tell Stoker to find some rags for you," she said, "and then you can wipe all that grease off the bicycle. And then wash your hands in the scullery and take your jersey off and give it to Stoker before you come into the house at all."

"Oh, mother! Oh, all right then."

Laura went into the kitchen and told Stoker to find some old cloths for Tony and see that he washed before he came into the house.

"Of course," said Tony's voice from the yard, addressing an invisible friend, "if people make one ungrease one's bike, they can't be surprised if it doesn't work properly."

At half-past seven Stoker rang the bell for supper. As there was no sound of Tony his mother went into the dining room and found him sitting in his chair with a pink, cheerful face. He was in his shirt, his sleeves rolled up to his shoulders. His hands were exquisitely clean, but his arms and shirt were nearly as dirty as his jersey had been.

"What have you been doing?" said his mother. "I thought I told you to get clean before you came in."

"I did, mother. I washed my hands like anything."

He exhibited his spotless hands with pride. His mother said nothing, but continued to eye him and his shirt with disfavor.

"Well, I couldn't help getting my shirt dirty," said Tony in an aggrieved voice. "I took off my jersey and gave it to Stoker, just as you told me to, so then of course the oil got on my shirt."

"But, you idiot, I didn't tell you take off your jersey till you had finished cleaning the bicycle. Now Stoker will have to wash the shirt as well. Go into the scullery and take off your shirt and wash your arms. And then go up and get a clean shirt. And hurry up," she added, as Tony rose with an ill grace.

But nature has seen to it that boys shall not be overdriven, by making it quite impossible for them to hurry or to concentrate over things that don't interest them. It was after a quarter to eight before Tony, shiningly clean, sat down to supper. All evening he was so angelic that his mother reproached herself bitterly for quick temper and fault finding. When he had finished his supper, he took his mother's hand, led her to the drawing room, pushed her into an arm chair, kissed her so hard that her face was nearly driven in, brought her the reading aloud book, and only interrupted her once, to ask if he could get his drawing things.

"Bedtime now, Tony," said Laura as she shut the book.

"Oh, mother! Mother, can I just show you what I have been drawing? I've done a new map of Morland with four dirt tracks in it. Look, there's one near Drippingham—you remember Drippingham, don't you, mother?—and three others. The biggest is twelve miles around and the smallest is four miles around. I shall let Dora come over from Dorland and look at them. I shall have a special chromium-plated bike and simply dash around them. I really need a stopwatch to time the rounds. Do you know how much a stopwatch costs, mother?"

"No."

"Well, anyway I shall save up and get one. There's a chap at school whose brother has a stopwatch. He's one of the little chaps, only seven and very nice. I help him with his Latin prep. sometimes. He is awfully funny, mother. He goes about making awfully funny faces. I wish you could see him. Mother, if I save up and buy a stopwatch, will you time me, or would it make you too tired?"

Laura was so touched by this sudden thoughtfulness that she nearly cried, but pulling herself together, she expressed willingness to time him as much as he liked; a willingness which was certainly increased by the extreme improbability of his ever possessing a stopwatch. When he had gone to bed she rang up the Vicarage and had a talk with Mrs. Gould about lubricating oil. Rose and Dora appeared to have come off more lightly than Tony in the matter of actual dirt, but the Vicar had been very angry and forbidden the garage to all three children, a piece of news that Laura was delighted to hear.

"Mother," shouted Tony from upstairs.

"What is it? Go to bed."

"I am, but I thought you liked me to say good night."

"Good night, darling. Oh, and Tony, Mr. Gould says none of you are to go into the garage again."

There was a brief silence, during which Tony was evidently considering this statement.

"In Morland," he said carelessly, "I have seven million garages and I go into all of them, so it really doesn't matter. Besides, mother, Mr. Gould has such rotten oil. Someone really ought to tell him that one doesn't keep lubricating oil for people to oil their bikes with. He simply seems to know nothing. Good night, mother."

CHAPTER 2

THE WISHING WELL

Tony was cleaning his bicycle in the yard, near the kitchen door. Cleaning is perhaps not quite the right word for the languishing dabs which he made from time to time at the framework of the machine, and such was Stoker's freely expressed opinion.

"Henry Brown'll have something to say to you, Master Tony, if you don't clean the bike no better than that. A lick and a promise, that's your idea. And pick up that lamp off the ground. You'll be putting your foot on it, and then where will you be?"

"You ride much better without a lamp," said Tony. "You see, if you have a lamp it makes everything else seem much darker. Animals don't need lamps at night. Their eyes get trained to see in the dark. My eyes are trained to seeing in the dark, Stokes. I bet you I could get from here to the Vicarage on the darkest night without a light. But if I had one I'd probably rush into a ditch or something."

"Animals don't need no lamps at night, seeing as they don't go about," retorted Stoker. "Lay down in the fields or the cowshed, that's what they do. Anyway, Master Tony, you know your mother said you wasn't to ride after dark."

"I know. But everyone rides without lights, at least all decent riders do. And if you tied a lantern around a dog's neck, what do you think would happen, Stokes? It would be quite dazzled and not know which way to go."

"Get its hair burnt off, more likely," said Stoker.

"But if it was alone in the dark," continued Tony, disregarding this interruption, "it would find its way anywhere by instinct. I bet if you put me anywhere around about sixty miles from here with the bike, in the middle of the night, I'd find my way home. I have a kind of instinct like a dog."

"That's more than anyone can tell," said Stoker. "You'd better get on with cleaning that bike, Master Tony."

Shortly after this Tony came into the room where his mother was writing, left the door open and stood balancing on one leg. Her attention having been drawn by this pantomime, Mrs. Morland put down her pencil and looked up.

"Well, what is it?" she asked.

"Oh, mother, could I take the bike down to the garage?"

"Why?"

"The pump won't work."

"Rubbish, Tony, the pump was all right yesterday."

"I know. But I've been pumping for simply hours and the back tire is much too flat to ride. It's very bad for bicycles to be ridden with flat tires. It cuts the inner tube to pieces and strains the rim of the wheel."

Laura got up and went down to the yard, followed by Tony.

"Now show me how it won't pump up," she said.

With a miserable despairing face Tony took the pump in a languid grasp and pushed it in and out two or three times. He then groaned and stood up exhausted.

"Ass," said his mother unsympathetically, "give it to me."

"Oh, very well."

Laura gave about a dozen pumps and felt the back tire.

"Hard as nails," she said briskly.

"I know," said Tony. "But as soon as I'm on the road it will go down again. I have to spend simply all my time pumping it up. That's why I was so late coming back from the station yesterday, that and the parcel I had to carry. Mother, it isn't good for racing bikes to have parcels on them, and this was such a huge parcel it made the back tire go right down."

"Why didn't you take a basket and carry it on the handle-bars then, as I told you?" said his mother.

"Oh, mother, I couldn't ride about with a basket. Everyone would stare at me. Oh, mother, Mrs. Gould is having a lunch picnic tomorrow at the Wishing Well, and can I go? And she wants you to come too."

"Yes, I should think so. I haven't anything special to do tomorrow. I'll tell Stoker to make a sandwich lunch for us and we'll start about half-past twelve. Does Mrs. Gould want me to fetch them?"

"No, mother; the Vicar doesn't want the car, that's why we are having a picnic."

"Then it will only be you and me in our car."

Tony's face fell.

"But, mother, I thought you would like me to go on the bike. Then you could go in Mrs. Gould's car, and it would be more of a rest for you than having to drive yourself," said Tony sanctimoniously. "Besides, it's really waste of money if I don't use the bike when you are paying Henry for it, isn't it?"

"But it's such a long way for you to ride, Tony," said his mother, weakly temporising, though she knew that defeat was inevitable.

"Oh, mother, it's only about six miles, and I can do that in no time. I can easily do twenty miles an hour. Besides, Rose and Dora will be so disappointed if I don't go on the bike. I promised they'd see me come whizzing along. I bet I can go faster than Mrs. Gould's car up Southbridge Hill, mother. Henry's bike is low geared, so it's splendid for hill climbing. I can go on the bike, can't I, mother?"

"But what about the tires? I thought you said they couldn't be pumped up."

"I know. But if I pump them up jolly hard before we start, and about ten times on the way, I dare say it will do," said Tony with gentle melancholy.

Mrs. Morland resigned herself, knowing that the expedition would be little but a cause of worry and anxiety, but with a vague feeling that

Tony ought to be allowed to do everything that frightened her, in case he became a milksop.

Next morning Tony came down to breakfast with a white Sunday shirt, a rather vulgar-looking striped tie, distinctly the worse for wear, and his hair unpleasantly slabbed down with the Butygloss Hair Fixative.

"Must you wear that tie, Tony?" said his mother, "and wouldn't a grey flannel shirt be nicer for riding?"

"Mother, I *couldn't* wear a flannel shirt to ride to Southbridge. People will be looking at me all the way. Besides, I thought you liked me to look tidy when I go out."

"So I do, but a flannel shirt looks just as tidy and much more suitable for riding. Anyway, do put on your school tie. This one looks like an old piece of string."

"I know. But it's a very good tie, mother. Don't you think people would like me in this tie, mother? I got it myself for one and sixpence halfpenny. Oh, mother, need I wear my school tie? I promised Rose and Dora that I'd let them see this tie, and they'll be awfully disappointed if I don't. What are we taking for lunch?"

"I don't know yet. I must go and see Stoker. You had better finish your breakfast and tidy up your playroom, because Stoker wants to clean it while we are out today."

"Oh, mother, need I? Mother, I'm going to make a new railway system with a dirt track for bike races in the middle of it. There will be a station called Dirt Track Halt. Could I have some earth from the garden to make a dirt track?"

"Certainly not."

"Then I just can't have a racecourse," said Tony reproachfully. "People can't be expected to bicycle on linoleum, mother. Couldn't I have just enough earth to make it look like a dirt track?"

"No, Tony. It would make far too much mess. Can't you say the linoleum is concrete? A concrete track like Brooklands would be splendid."

"But, mother, you don't understand. Bicycling is quite different. At my dirt track at Drippingham—"

But his mother, who had been edging towards the door, escaped into the kitchen, leaving Tony to finish his breakfast and meditate on the system of tyranny which made one have to tidy one's playroom and forbade one to bring earth into it.

At twelve o'clock Tony, still wearing his white shirt and striped tie, set off for the Wishing Well. His plan to ride beside the car, dazzling the little girls by feats of bicyclemanship, had been squashed by Laura. Quite unimpressed by his repeated assertions that he could go twice as fast as Mrs. Gould's car, she packed him off ahead of the Vicarage party. She felt that it would be happier for her on the whole to anticipate discovering his mangled corpse by the road than to imagine the corpse on the road behind her, while the distance between them increased rapidly.

Stoker had worked off some of her feelings towards the Vicarage cook by preparing a lunch which would have done credit to Fortnum and Mason. As Mrs. Gould drove up to the house, with Rose and Dora jiggling about in the back seat, Stoker came to the front door, carrying a large basket.

"Good morning, Stoker," said Mrs. Gould.

"Morning," said Stoker. "I thought you mightn't have enough for lunch, so I've put you up something as you *can* eat."

"What is it, Stoker?" shrieked the two little girls.

"Something you wouldn't get at home," said Stoker darkly.

"Is it jam and ham and beer in the bottle and sherry and sham?" said Rose eagerly.

"What on earth are you talking about?" asked Laura, coming out of the house.

"It's a lovely poem of Stoker's, Mrs. Morland. She told it us the day we all had tea in the kitchen when you were out."

"Do tell me the rest of it," urged Laura.

Rose went pink with pleasure and embarrassment, but appeared to be struck dumb. Then flinging her arms around her mother's neck she whispered into her ear.

"Rose wants you to say it, Stoker," said Mrs. Gould.

Stoker smiled indulgently and shook her head.

"Go on, Rose," said Laura, suddenly envisaging Tony under the wheels of a motor coach, and anxious to start.

"Go on, Rose," said Dora, "or I'll say it."

Stimulated by this threat, Rose hastily gabbled in a high voice:

"We'd jam and we'd ham,
We'd beer in the bottle and sherry and cham,
And never in your life did you see such a jam
    As there was when we all sat down.
We'd forks and we'd knives,
And we pegged away like working for our lives.
With the girls and boys and the fellows and
    their wives,
    We ate up half the town."

"That's right," said Stoker approvingly. "Miss Rose doesn't recite too bad. I used to be a great one for reciting myself when I was a girl. You had ought to have heard me on the platform at the socials."

"I wish I had," said Mrs. Gould.

"Thank you, Rose," said Laura, getting into the front seat beside Mrs. Gould. "Good-bye, Stoker. We'll probably be back to tea."

"Please yourselves," said Stoker, and departed into the house whistling loudly.

No sooner had they started than both little girls rattled off a fire of questions about Tony's bicycling exploits.

"I don't know," said his mother, "but I shouldn't think he could go at forty miles an hour, and I shouldn't think he could ride up Southbridge Hill, or race the motor coach. But when we find him we'll ask him to tell us. I shall be so glad when the bicycle is broken," she added plaintively to Mrs. Gould, "even if I have to pay Henry Brown for a new one. You can't think how agitating it is to have Tony all over the country, always expecting to be rung up and told he has had his arms and legs cut off, or is awaiting identification at the mortuary. But he always breaks everything he has sooner or later, so I hope he will break the bicycle soon."

"Well, we are sure to see him before we get to the picnic," said Mrs. Gould, far too carelessly. "I told him to go straight to the Wishing Well at the end of the Long Ponds. We shall catch him up long before then."

Meanwhile Tony had been having a delightful ride. He had found it difficult to make up his mind whether to ride at great speed through the village, so raising fear and admiration in the hearts of beholders, or to ride very slowly, frequently turning around in the road, which would in its turn compel admiration, though not awe. This second method also had the advantage of enabling one to show off to practically all one's friends.

Scorching up the little drive, head down over the handles, Tony turned the corner into the road too rapidly, skidded on the tarmac, and fell off. He picked himself up with a cross expression on his soft face, remounted and rode on.

Mr. Brown of the garage was standing by his petrol pumps talking to Dr. Ford when Tony dashed up, applied both brakes violently, got off and stood breathing loudly.

"Well, Tony," said Dr. Ford, "how's the bicycle?"

"All right, sir," said Tony briefly. "Oh, Mr. Brown, I just fell off once and the mudguard got all on one side. People make such rotten mudguards. Of course a *real* racing bike oughtn't to have mudguards at all. They reduce speed. Dr. Ford, what do you think is the fastest a racing bike could go? I bet I could speed at about forty if you paced me in your car."

"If I hadn't any patients I might consider it," said the doctor, getting into his car. "Goodbye, Tony; don't break your neck today, because I have a long consultation at Southbridge."

"Dr. Ford doesn't seem to understand," said Tony to Mr. Brown and a large imaginary audience, "that one doesn't break one's neck on a racing bike. Anyone who can ride decently never hurt themselves when they fall off. You just fall properly. Of course, if people will put rotten mudguards on bikes they naturally get bent. Do you think you could straighten it, Mr. Brown?"

"Don't you go falling off again," said Mr. Brown when the job was done. "That bike wasn't made to be thrown about."

"I know. But I didn't fall off. I was just coming around the corner rather fast—I can go round corners at a terrific angle—and it fell over."

Tony remounted and rode on in a triumphant progress. Fortune was so far on his side that most of his friends were in their front gardens or at their shop doors. He was able to wave his hand to Mrs. Mallow outside the surgery and to Mr. Reid outside the shop, before he slowed down near the Vicarage. Rose and Dora, who were standing at the gate waiting for their mother to bring the car around, greeted him with admiring shrieks. Tony waved a lordly hand, wobbled perilously, and came rather uncomfortably to rest against the Vicarage garden wall.

"Did you see me wave my hand?" he asked. "I can ride with one hand just as easily as with two. In fact I really don't need to hold the handle bars at all. I can't think why people have handle bars. Anyone could ride without them; you just have to balance. Wait till you see me simply dashing down the Southbridge Hill on the way home, with my hands in my pockets. I expect I'll have to wait for hours for you at the Wishing Well. I'll be doing about twenty-five all the way."

"Dorland *has* got a dirt track," said Dora suddenly.

"I know," said Tony. "But there isn't really one, because I told you they aren't invented yet. Anyway, it probably isn't a proper dirt track at all. What do you have on it?"

"Dirt," said Dora decidedly.

"What sort of dirt?"

"The proper sort."

"Well, it can't be the proper sort, because the right dirt is only in Morland. I have an enormous quarry for dirt. The Dorland kind is all wrong; in fact, you couldn't bicycle on it. Your dirt track is probably just concrete."

"Is there a dirt track at Rosebush?" asked Rose anxiously.

"No. But you can come and see me ride on mine, and Dora can come too. I'll send a Morland steamer to fetch her."

"Thank you," said both little girls rapturously.

"Now you can see me start," said Tony, pushing himself away from the wall.

"Wave your hand, Tony," shrieked Dora.

Tony raised a hand in a brief uninterested salute and disappeared around the corner. The tarmac road was in good condition, and he rode happily along between the hedges, making the noises of a motor bicycle as he went. The road to the Wishing Well lay along a ridge, dipped to a stream, and then rose to Southbridge Hill, famous for its motor tests. The winding descent to the little River Rising was successfully negotiated, but just as Tony was preparing to take off across the bridge for the upward climb on the other side he remembered a certain little spit of meadow that stuck out into the stream. For some time it had been in his mind to cut a canal across this isthmus, so making an island of his own, and here was a heaven-sent opportunity with no grownups to interfere. Slackening speed, he hurled himself to the ground, put the bicycle in the ditch, and went down to the waterside. A canal a couple of feet long would do the job, if one had anything to dig with. A broken piece of fencing made a good temporary spade. Tony shook off his jacket, turned his shirt sleeves up to the shoulder and his stockings down over his boots, and was soon so absorbed in the work in hand that he never noticed the Vicarage car go by. Nor did his unsuspecting mother notice the bicycle lying in the ditch among last year's bracken.

The canal was unexpectedly difficult. Mud and sand poured in as fast as one dug, silting up the channel. Roots impeded one's progress, squelchy mud came up over one's shoes, but Tony dug resolutely till he came to a piece of masonry, apparently the end of an old drain.

"Of course people would put concrete just where people want to dig," he said aloud in an indignant voice. "Simply wasting a person's time. Oh, well, if people don't *want* canals they needn't have them."

He stood up, threw his spade into the steam, watched it until it ran ashore in an eddy, and returned to his bicycle. His plan of whizzing up

Southbridge Hill was rather damped by the necessity of going back a couple of hundred yards to get up speed for the final dash. He pedalled with dogged determination up the road by which he had come, and when he could push on no further turned around and dashed downhill. The impetus carried him a short way up the steep ascent on the other side, but his strength was not enough to take him up to the top. In spite of furious pressure exerted with the whole weight of his body, first on one pedal and then on the other, in spite of veering and tacking across the road, he was obliged to dismount and push his bicycle to the top of the hill. Here he got on again, rode a little way along the road, and turned off into the woods by the Long Ponds.

The Vicarage car had got to the Wishing Well just about the time when Tony was attempting the hill. Laura, who had been controlling herself very well on the journey, looked anxiously around, but saw no sign of her son.

"Where is Tony?" said Rose.

"I expect he is somewhere about," said Mrs. Gould, comfortably aware that it was not her child who was missing. "You and Dora go and look for him while we get lunch ready."

The little girls wandered off. Mrs. Morland helped Mrs. Gould to unpack, but was feeling sick with fear. Quite obviously Tony had either been run over on the way and picked up by a passing motorist and was now unconscious in Southbridge Hospital or he had ridden on so far ahead that he had lost his way and would probably never be heard of again.

"What a lovely lunch Stoker has made," said Mrs. Gould a little enviously.

"What? Oh, yes," said Laura. "You don't think we could possibly have passed Tony on the road, do you?"

"We would have seen him if we had. I expect he is just exploring a bit," said Mrs. Gould with hateful calm.

A bicycle bell was heard. Laura was just calling herself an idiot for worrying so unnecessarily when a man and a girl on a tandem passed them and disappeared into the woods. She felt more mortally sick than before, and knew that she would cry on the slightest provocation. The lunch was all laid out and Mrs. Gould shouted for Rose and Dora, who almost immediately appeared.

"Did you see Tony?" said their mother carelessly. "Oh, well, he can't be far off. We'll begin lunch and he can join in when he comes."

For the first time in her life Laura hated the Vicar's wife, and formed in her mind contemptuous remarks about people who only have girls. It was now so evident that Tony was in hospital, urgently needing her but unable to explain who he was, that her eyes began to swim. Already she was following a small coffin to the churchyard, supported by her publisher, Adrian Coates, on one side and her old friend, George Knox, the famous biographer, on the other. Already, repulsing their anxious offers of help and sympathy, she remained alone by the newly filled grave in the gathering twilight. A doubt passed through her mind as to whether people were buried at twilight: didn't one have to be buried before three o'clock, or was that only for weddings? But putting this doubt aside, she fell into a miserable ecstasy, contemplating the sable robed figure standing mute by a child's grave, from which she was only roused by the little girls' shouts of "Tony, Tony."

"Did you ride all the way up the Southbridge Hill?" asked Dora, as he got off the bicycle.

"Practically."

"Did you really do twenty-five?" asked Rose.

"I averaged about twenty-five," said Tony carelessly.

"Why are you so late?" asked his mother. "You started long before we did."

"I know. Oh, mother, did Stoker give us sausage rolls? I could eat about twenty."

"Yes," said his mother. "But what were you doing? And why are your shoes all muddy? And do pull those stockings up."

"Well, mother," said Tony, ignoring the question of mud, "if one has a rotten pump and a rotten mudguard, you can't expect to get along fast all the time. If you had let me ride behind the motor I could have speeded all the way, but anyone would tell you that you can't keep up a record speed by yourself."

Lunch proceeded. Tony gave great satisfaction to Rose and Dora by cramming two sausage rolls into his mouth at once. He then gave several dull and pointless imitations of M. Dubois, Mr. Prothero, and other school characters, to which the little girls listened with rapt attention.

"'Oh, I die for food,'" Tony declaimed, as his mother passed around a plate of meringues.

"'Here I lie down and measure out my grave.'"

"What?" said Mrs. Gould, much startled.

"It's only *As You Like It*," said Laura. "Tony's school are doing it next term.

"Oh, Tony, are you really acting?" said Rose adoringly.

"What are you?" said Dora.

"Adam, of course."

"Who is that?"

"Haven't you read any Shakespeare?" said Tony pityingly. "But I dare say no one has ever heard of Shakespeare in Dorland."

"Yes, they have."

"Well, you don't know much about him if you don't know that Adam is a very important person in *As You Like It*. They wouldn't have anyone to do Adam who wasn't pretty good. I don't know how it is, but when I speak my voice always seems to sound better than the other chap's. Somehow their voices sound quite unfavorable compared with mine. I expect I have a kind of gift for the stage."

"I'd like to see you act," said Dora. "I expect you'd forget your part."

"I couldn't. I know all my own part and everyone else's too, I don't know why, but somehow I seem to acquire all the parts. I could act *As You Like It* all through by myself. I'll tell you what, we'll act it at my theater in Morland. There isn't a theater in Dorland," he added hastily, seeing Dora about to speak; "only a cinema, so you can't act it there. I expect I'll get quite a lot of applause."

Mrs. Morland, who had been discussing the Women's Institute

with Mrs. Gould, now called out to Tony to help in clearing away the remains of lunch.

"Oh, mother, need I? We've only just finished and I am quite ready to rest."

"Get on with the job, Tony," said his mother unkindly. "You're not so old as all that."

"'Though I look old'," remarked Tony getting up, "'yet am I strong and lusty;

For in my youth I never did apply

Hot and rebellious liquors in my blood,

Nor did not with unbashful forehead woo

The means of weakness and debility.'"

"That's enough," said his mother hastily, as her son's ringing accents filled the clearing where they sat. "Clear away, and then you can each have a penny to drop into the Wishing Well."

The Wishing Well was a little bubbling spring with a sandy bottom, overhung by a natural arch of stone. Custom decreed that tribute must be paid with a coin or a pin, which ensured the fulfillment of one's wish.

"You wish first," said Mrs. Morland to the Vicar's wife, who dropped a pin into the water and silently wished for a new kitchen range. Mrs. Morland followed, with a silent prayer for Tony to get home safely and the bicycle to be broken. With a good deal of giggling and pushing the three children dropped their pennies in.

"What did you wish?" asked Rose of Dora.

"Well, what did *you* wish?"

"You won't get your wish if you tell it," said Rose.

"Oh, Rose, I didn't think you would be so supersistious," said Tony.

"You mean superstitious," said Rose, from the altitude of fourteen.

"I know. But it's stupid to be supersistious. I wished I could have a dirt track in the garden. I dare say I shall, too. What did you wish?"

"I wished to see *As You Like It*," said Rose self-consciously.

"Good for you," said Tony briefly.

"Oh, Rose," said Dora, "that was my wish."

"That's all right," said Tony. "You can both come to the Morland Theater Royal."

"But we meant really acted, at your school."

"I dare say I can fix that for you."

Both little girls bent admiring grateful glances on their companion. All three then besieged the mothers with questions about what they had wished. At first they would not tell, but a compromise was arrived at by which Mrs. Gould was to tell hers and Mrs. Morland to keep it secret. The result would show whether the wishing well really favored reticence. Mrs. Gould's choice of a kitchen range roused no interest among the children, and the subject dropped.

When the time came to go home Laura begged Mrs. Gould to drive very slowly, or halt frequently, so that Tony could keep up on his bicycle.

"I simply couldn't stand another hour of anxiety," she said earnestly.

Her plan was accordingly adopted, and Tony had the pleasure of showing off to his audience and keeping them in fits of admiring giggles by such brilliant jokes as pretending to fall off, or wobbling his front wheel violently. When they came to the Southbridge Hill he shot rapidly ahead and in spite of his mother's expostulations, vanished from their sight.

"Catch him, mummy, catch him," shrieked Rose and Dora in chorus. Mrs. Morland turned such an agonized face to her friend that Mrs. Gould drove down the hill a good deal faster than she meant to. At the bottom Tony was sitting on the bank, gloomily rubbing one leg, the bicycle lying at his feet.

"Are you all right?" asked Mrs. Gould, stopping the car.

Tony merely groaned and went on rubbing his leg.

"Don't be an ass, Tony," said his mother with the anger of fright. "What idiot's trick have you been up to now?"

"If people will make back brakes that won't work properly," said Tony, ceasing his groans for a moment, "of course people will have accidents."

"What's wrong with your leg?" asked his mother, getting out of the car. "It's nothing but a few scratches, Tony."

"I know. But I expect I'll get blood poisoning. I didn't put my iodine pencil in this jacket. You always ought to put iodine on cuts to prevent germs getting in."

"That's enough," said his unsympathetic mother. "Get up and stop that noise and come home."

Tony rose and limped to his bicycle. He mounted with a very good imitation of a rheumatic octogenarian, but in a moment he was off again, letting the bicycle fall heavily on its side.

"It's no good," he said despairingly. "If they make such rotten brakes that they get out of order and scrape the back rim all the time, they can't expect a person to ride."

It was only too true. The brakes, bent from their proper position, were bearing heavily on the rim of the back wheel, making progress slow and difficult.

"All right," said Laura, who mysteriously enough seemed to be in an excellent temper. "Get in, Tony, and we'll take the bicycle to Mr. Brown."

Still groaning, Tony climbed into the back seat with the little girls. The bicycle was packed in on their legs and in a few moments they drew up at Mr. Brown's garage.

Mr. Brown came out, raised his eyebrows, and took the bicycle out of the car. Laura asked him to cast an eye over it and say what was wrong.

"I expect it's a defect in the steel," said Tony. "That's the way all the worst accidents happen. Is it a defect in the steel, Mr. Brown?"

"That's right," said Mr. Brown, concluding his examination. "The back fork is nearly fractured, Mrs. Morland. Master Tony's come off easy. He might have broke his neck."

Concealing her intense pleasure, Mrs. Morland asked what the repairs would cost. Mr. Brown expressed the opinion that the defect was so serious that the makers would be bound to replace the back fork, under the guarantee given at the time of purchase.

"I'll just see Henry about it, Mrs. Morland," he said, "but I'm pretty sure it's all right."

"And how long will it take?" asked Laura, staking her happiness on one throw. Mr. Brown was of the opinion that Master Tony wouldn't be likely to get it back before the end of the holidays.

"Well, that's very sad," said Laura, her heart lighter than it had been for many days. "If there is anything to pay you must let me know. Goodbye."

Mrs. Gould drove on to the Morlands' house, Tony in the back seat expounding to the girls what feats he would have performed if the bicycle had not broken down.

"If the car hadn't been so slow you'd have seen me going down Southbridge Hill like lightning," he said. "I'd have gone up the hill on the other side as easily as winking and got home hours before you. I don't know how it is, but I have a sort of instinct for bikes. I had an instinct that there was a defect somewhere in it. Anyone who knows about steel knows when there is a defect. I expect the steel wasn't made properly. In Morland the bikes are all made of aluminum. I don't think much of these makers if they can't mend a bicycle before the end of the holidays. At my works in Morland they can mend a bike in twenty-four hours, whatever it is."

"So they can in Dorland," said Dora.

"I know. But they can't, because they haven't got proper plant. I have a wonderful instinct about plant. If I had a lathe and a welding machine I could mend anything."

The car drew up at Mrs. Morland's drive and she got out.

"Goodbye," she said to Mrs. Gould, "and thank you for a lovely picnic. I haven't been so happy for days as today. Goodbye, Rose; goodbye, Dora; come again soon."

"Goodbye, Tony," called the little girls.

Tony nodded at them and went around to the kitchen door.

"Hello, Stokes," he said, entering the kitchen. "The bike's smashed. There was a defect in the steel. If I hadn't had an instinct to get off I'd have been killed."

"Not you," said Stoker robustly.

"I wish I had a bike of my own," said Tony, "but mother won't let me have one till my legs are longer. Some of the chaps at school are much younger than me, but they have longer legs. I'll tell you what, Stokes. The tall ones are very good at games, but I can beat them easily at work. Some of the little short ones that are younger than me are awfully good at their work, but they don't seem to have much sense for games. I expect they use up all their strength in swotting. I don't know why, but I seem to be about fifty-fifty, because I'm good at games and good at work."

"Didn't see no prizes last term," said Stoker, who was putting tea on a tray.

"I know. The chaps that are best at work don't always win the prizes. If I wasn't so good at work I dare say my legs would grow a bit longer."

"I dare say if you didn't talk to much your tongue would get a bit longer," said Stoker. "You'll wear it out one of these fine days."

"I know. But really, Stokes," said Tony, following her into the drawing room, "if I didn't work so hard with my brain I would grow faster. Mother, do you think if I didn't do Greek my legs would get any longer? All the chaps who are good at Greek are very short."

"Come and have your tea," said his mother. "That was a lovely lunch you gave us, Stoker. We had it at the Wishing Well."

"Get your wish?" asked Stoker. "I never got mine.

"Was that because you told it?" asked Tony.

Stoker nodded portentously and left the room.

After eating a heavy tea in comparative silence, Tony rushed upstairs and came down again with something in his hand.

"What's that?" asked his mother.

"My iodine pencil, mother. Don't you want me not to get infection with germs? You don't remember that I got my leg cut when the bike had defective steel at the bottom of the hill."

As he spoke he dropped the glass pencil on the floor.

"Oh, did you get your wish, mother?" he said, walking on the pencil and crushing glass and iodine into the carpet.

"Yes, I did. Oh, Tony, look at the mess you've made."

"I know. If people will make iodine pencils of such weak glass, mother, one can't help breaking them."

"You needn't have walked on it, though," said his mother mildly. "Give me a hug, and then go and tell Stoker to come and clean up the carpet."

Tony hugged his mother long and throttlingly, his arms tight around her neck, her arms enfolding him. Then he went off to find Stoker.

Mrs. Morland looked placidly at the mess and stain which would mark her carpet forever. Stoker, coming in with broom and wet cloth, could not understand why her mistress took the disaster so lightly. What she did not know was that Laura still felt in her arms Tony's hard, beloved, uncaring little body; and that she had got her wish.

11

THE HALF-TERM HOLIDAY

CHAPTER I
THE HALF-TERM HOLIDAY

This Monday in June was a half-term holiday. Parents could come to the school and take their sons out for the day, or spend the day at the school with them. Laura Morland, who was an old friend of the headmaster and his wife, had arranged to drive over from High Rising and take her youngest son out to lunch and later have tea with Mrs. Birkett.

On Sunday night Tony had made a special plan with the elder Fairweather, the captain of the boxing, who slept in the lower dormitory. Fairweather was to rouse Master Wesendonck, who slept next to him, long before dawn. Fairweather and Master Wesendonck were then to go softly upstairs, not waking matron or Mr. Ferris, the house master, who slept near the boys, and spend a delightful hour in Tony's cubicle before slipping back to their beds again. Tony had been for two terms the happy tenant of a cubicle to himself, owing to being a senior monitor, and was looking forward with disgust and scorn to the Easter term next year, when he would be moved across to the Upper School and have to start life again in a dormitory. It was, as he often explained to his mother, or anyone else who cared to listen to him or could not get away from him, impossible to sleep in a dormitory. The mere fact that a jet of gas, turned down to its lowest point, was left alight at one end of the long room, so seared the eyeballs that sleep was out of the question.

"One can't possibly go to sleep, mother," said Tony, before he went back to school, "unless it's perfectly dark. You see, one's eyelids are very thin, and even when they are shut the light comes through. If you have ever noticed, if you look at the sun with your eyes shut there is a kind of red light everywhere. Did you know that, mother?"

"I did."

"Well, it's just like that when the gas is left on. I have a kind of light in my eyes all night, so I don't ever get to sleep till about one o'clock. One ought to be in the dark if one is to go to sleep, like an animal."

"What about owls," said Laura, "and all the animals that prowl about at night and sleep in the day?"

"Well, mother, they have burrows, or put their heads under their wings."

"You looked very comfortable in your burrow under the bed clothes this morning, Tony, when I came in to wake you, and you had left the electric light on all night."

"I know. Mother, could I have that American stamp off your letter?"

Laura handed him the envelope. He removed the stamp with a large and masterful gesture, tearing off a corner as he did so, rammed it into an already bulging pocket, and continued:

"Besides, mother, if you knew you had to get up at half-past seven when a bell rings, you wouldn't be able to stay asleep in the morning. I have a kind of instinct about the bell, so that I only sleep in a miserable kind of way, waiting for the bell to ring. I hardly ever get a good night's rest, mother."

"I wish your instinct would tell you when the breakfast bell is going to ring at home," said Laura, rather tartly. "Stoker can't keep breakfast hot for you all the morning."

But this statement, so Tony's instinct told him, was untrue.

On the Monday morning, from which we have somehow wandered, Fairweather had succeeded in waking himself up at five a.m. With infinite precaution he put on his dressing gown and slippers and tiptoed to Master Wesendonck's bed. That gentleman was curled up in a tight ball with his head under the bedclothes and showed no disposition to be roused. In fact, the indignant if unconscious grunt that he gave when touched, frightened Fairweather so much that he gave up all hope of waking his confederate and stole out of the room alone. Luckily Mr. Ferris was a heavy sleeper and the passage and staircase were very solid, without any loose or creaking boards, so Fairweather arrived safely at Tony's door and let himself in. His only fear was that Tony might be asleep, in which case it might be difficult to rouse him without also waking the matron, but Tony was wide awake, with his stamp collection spread out on his bed.

"Hello, Fairy," said Tony, "where's the Donk?"

"Fast asleep, the silly ass. I tried to wake him up, but he made such a row I thought old Ferret would hear, so I had to leave him. Have you got a Belgium one for King Albert's death?" said Fairweather, opening a small purse crammed with stamps.

"No, but I've got some jolly decent China ones that my brother who's on the China station sent me."

"Where is the China station?" asked Fairweather, who was so bad at lessons that only his position as a brilliant athlete and captain of boxing kept him in any class at all.

"You don't seem to know much geography," said Tony contemptuously.

"Well, where is it then?"

"In China, of course."

"Isn't your brother a midshipman?"

"Yes."

"Well, why is he in a station? I bet he's only a railway porter."

"Well, he isn't, so there. The China station is too difficult to explain to you if you don't know any geography. Have you ever heard of a railhead?"

"No."

Tony shrugged his shoulders and decided to let the matter drop.

The little boys then compared stamps and made exchanges. By the time that a number of dirty, torn and crumpled stamps had changed hands, both amateurs were satisfied. The difficulties of bargaining were increased by the necessity of speaking in whispers, which also brought on violent fits of giggles that had to be stifled in pillows and dressing gowns, so the whole affair, though well worth while, was very exhausting.

Presently Fairweather asked the time, but Tony had broken his watch again.

"Lean out of the window," said Tony, "and you'll see the school clock."

Fairweather opened the window at the bottom and put his head out.

"I say," he whispered loudly, "there's a wasp crawling about on the window sill. It's the first I've seen."

"Kill it," said Tony. "It's probably a queen wasp and it will have about a million young wasps. Every queen wasp has so many young wasps that if they all had children too the world would be quite solid with wasps, like wasp jam. I say, Fairy, wouldn't wasp jam be a ripping idea? I'd give a pot of wasp jam to matron and old Prothero, and they'd all swell up inside and die."

At this pleasant thought both little boys had the giggles again.

"Go on, you ass," said Tony, "whang the beastly thing. Here's my slipper—catch."

Tony threw his bedroom slipper vaguely in Fairweather's direction. Fairweather made a grab at it and missed. The slipper went straight out of the window and disappeared. The little boys looked at each other.

"I can see it," said Fairweather, leaning out of the window, "it's bang under old Birky's study window. Gosh, won't he go off pop when he sees it."

"Your fault, anyway," said Tony. "You can't even whang a wasp. Wait a minute. I'll show you."

He got out of bed, took a hairbrush and approached the window. The wasp was still crawling about on the window sill, stopping from time to time to open its unpleasant face down the middle and taste something sticky on the woodwork.

"Look, Fairy," said Tony, nudging his friend, "that's where I split the Butygloss Hair Fixative. The wasp's eating Hair Fixative."

"Great ass," said Fairweather scornfully. "He'll come out all over hairs like a caterpillar. I'll squelch him with my handkerchief."

"No, you won't, it's my wasp," said Tony, raising the hairbrush for the fatal blow.

Fairweather dropped his handkerchief, grabbed at Tony's brush and got possession of it. After a hot tussle Fairweather, finding Tony too strong for him, threw the hairbrush desperately from him, sooner than let it fall into the enemy's hands. It hurtled through a pane of glass and flew out of the window. The noise of the breaking glass was extremely sobering, and both little boys stood frozen in horror. This was just the kind of occasion on which matron, vengefully attired in an unbecoming boudoir cap, a blue flannel dressing gown and red bedroom slippers was apt to make an entirely unwanted appeared. It was only ten days ago that Tony and Master Wesendonck had put their pillow cases over their heads and acted an impromptu play about ghosts to a giggling selection of friends after lights were out. Matron's entrance, her chilly reception of their efforts and her very mean and sneaking report to Mr. Ferris had not been forgotten.

"You've done it now," said Tony, in gloomy triumph.

Fairweather tied the cord of his dressing gown more tightly around him to hearten himself and said he had better go back to the lower dormitory, in case the Ferret had woken up. It would be a pity, he said, to disturb the Ferret. Tony thought of a very good joke about the Ferret being ratty, but was too depressed to make use of it at the moment, so he got back into bed, and so far succeeded in forgetting his troubles that he was asleep again in five minutes.

After breakfast Tony sauntered about the house with his hands in his pockets till he found Edward, the school odd-man. In the elaborate system of school intrigue, which was the joy and interest of the boys, Edward was, on the whole, against the masters and the matron. Mr. Birkett, the headmaster, was tolerated on account of his wife, for whom Edward had a deep admiration, but all other masters he heartily disliked, especially Mr. Ferris and Mr. Prothero, for no reason

at all, except that they had not been in the war, an indulgence which
Mr. Ferris' youth and Mr. Prothero's age had put entirely out of the
question. With the matron Edward was on the worst of terms. As
matron was deeply resentful of Mr. Ferris, because as house master he
had authority over the dormitories, and Mr. Ferris, while outwardly in
command, was perpetually being reminded in ingenious ways that he
was as dirt compared with someone who had been in the house when
he was only a miserable lower school boy, Edward was able to indulge
in the balance of power, his chief weapons being complete control
over the cleaning of all shoes and a gift for repairing wireless sets.
These benefits he bestowed or withheld according to the state which
matron or Mr. Ferris occupied in his regard at the moment.

When Tony found him Edward was sitting in a place called the
boot hole, polishing a number of battered, down-trodden shoes
which it was his pride to keep in as good repair as possible. In addition
to his other gifts, he was an accomplished cobbler, a trade which he
had picked up, with many others, in the army. When he saw Tony he
held up a pair of cricket boots with the figures one nine marked in
little brass tacks on the soles.

"That's you, Morland, nineteen," he said. "Half the studs gone
again, and where's your laces?"

"In Mr. Prothero's room."

"That's not the place for laces."

"I know. But I was only practicing scout knots with them while I
was doing a bit of Ovid, and old Prothero took them away. Of course,
if people don't want one to learn one's scout knots properly, they
needn't. I bet Mr. Ferris would go off pop if he knew old Prothero
wouldn't let me practice my knots. Mr. Ferris is taking the scouts to
camp next weekend so we've all got to do our knots. He'll be pretty
sick about old Prothero."

"A month in the trenches would do Mr. Prothero a lot of good,"
said Edward, who had the single-hearted belief that the army was the
only cure for every shortcoming. "I've got a pair of laces somewhere,
I'll put in your boots. I don't know what you mother'll have to say to

the bill for repairs this term. What have you been doing to get the studs off like that?"

"I was only trying to scrape my feet on the scraper by the boarding house door. Matron doesn't like us to come in with dirt on our boots."

"Matron's an old woman," said Edward.

"I know. I expect she's about eighty-five. I say, Edward, you haven't seen my bedroom slipper, have you?"

Edward looked up from his polishing in surprise.

"You see," said Tony, "I was only trying to kill a wasp this morning and the beastly thing got out of the window."

"Best place for it. Don't you go trying to kill wasps, Morland; they always get the best of it."

"I know. I don't mean the wasp, Edward, I mean the slipper. It just went out of the window. And then my hairbrush went too. It was about six o'clock a.m. in the morning."

"And what were you doing at the window at six o'clock?"

"Nothing."

"Oh, yes, you were. Let's hear all about it, and I might be able to get the brush back before the gardeners come around."

"It was only Fairweather and me swopping stamps, and there was a wasp on the window sill and I threw my slipper at him for him to whang the wasp with and the silly ass missed it and it went out of the window. And then he wanted to kill the wasp with a hairbrush, and it was my wasp, so the hairbrush fell out of the window. It was jolly lucky matron didn't hear the glass break."

"It's jolly lucky you don't get some of the canings you deserve, Morland," said Edward. "Cut along now and I'll have a look for the brush."

Tony went off to find Fairweather. On his way through the boarding house his attention was attracted by a sound of brawling on the upper landing. He went up to look into the matter and found that the brawl consisted of Mr. Ferris and matron, with Master Wesendonck holding a watching brief. Matron had found the window broken in Tony's cubicle, and a very dirty handkerchief which wasn't Tony's. The handkerchief had been so often to the laundry, though not recently, that the name on it was illegible, but matron had deduced, purely on suspicion and previous conviction, that it belonged to a lower dormitory boy, probably Master Wesendonck. She had therefore caught and questioned Master Wesendonck, whose innocence did not prevent him showing every sign of guilty confusion. Mr. Ferris, passing by, had gone to enquire into the noise and had been justly indignant of matron's suspicion of one of his lower dormitory boys.

"Really, matron," he was saying in a high angry voice as Tony came up, "this is preposterous. It is absolutely impossible for any of the boys to leave my dormitory without my knowledge. Wesendonck was still asleep when I got up this morning. It is just as likely that one of your boys was in Morland's cubicle. I have more than once had occasion to complain of the want of discipline in the upper dormitory, and if this sort of things goes on I shall have to sleep upstairs myself."

"Well, I'm sure, Mr. Ferris," said matron, red with indignation, "I don't know what you're talking about. Thirty years I've been here and never such a thing said before. My boys upstairs are all like lambs."

"Here's one of the lambs," said Mr. Ferris, catching sight of Tony. "Morland, did you break that window in your cubicle?"

Under normal circumstances, that is to say if he had broken it, Tony's procedure would have been to say, "Window, sir? What window?" and so by divagations impede the course of justice till he got fifty lines for general imbecility instead of the heavier punishment for breaking a pane. But on this occasion fate had so played into his hands that truth was his best friend. His blue eyes fixed with conscious rectitude on his housemaster's face, he kicked one foot with the other and said, "No, sir."

"That's what you say," said Mr. Ferris rudely, "but you aren't usually a liar and I'll believe you. Was Wesendonck up in your cubicle this morning?"

"Oh no, sir. He's not been up since the time you told him not to, sir," said Tony virtuously. "Have you, Donk?"

Master Wesendonck shook his head.

"Well, matron," said Mr. Ferris, in the voice he intended to end discussions with when he was a headmaster, "I hope you are satisfied that the lower dormitory is blameless in this affair. I shall be obliged if you will refrain in future from bringing baseless allegations against my boys."

He walked off with dignity, followed by Master Wesendonck.

"Was one of the upper dormitory boys in your cubicle this morning, Morland?" asked matron, pursuing her inquisition.

Truth was again, incredibly, his friend.

"An upper dorm boy? In my cubicle? Oh no, matron, honestly not."

"Then who broke the window if you didn't?"

"Perhaps the glass was a bit loose and it got broken of itself," said Tony hopefully.

By this time they were outside the door of Tony's cubicle. Matron followed him in to complain about life in general and housemasters in particular, with special reference to the strain which their impertinence and incompetence put upon her physical and moral system. Under cover of her lamentations Tony put his one bedroom slipper neatly away with his other shoes and then dismissed the whole subject from his mind.

When Laura drove up a few minutes later she found Edward poking about among the shrubs outside the schoolhouse. He smiled at her in a mysterious way, slipped something into his pocket, saluted and went off. Laura was shown into the parents' waiting room, and shortly afterwards Tony, accompanied by Master Wesendonck, appeared and pushed his cheek at her.

"I thought we would go to Barchester and have lunch at an hotel for a treat," said Laura, "and then see the cathedral."

"Oh, mother, need we see the cathedral?"

"Yes, we need. Mr. Knox is with me, and he particularly wants to see it because of something he is writing a book about, so come on."

Tony, reflecting that Mr. Knox would probably be good for a tip, made no further objections. He had, in fact, no particular prejudice against cathedrals, and vastly enjoyed climbing up corkscrew staircases, but one's natural reaction to anything a mother suggests is of course to want to do something else. It is simply a question of self-respect. As they crossed the hall matron came hurriedly down-stairs, nearly colliding with Edward as he emerged from the servants' quarters.

"Sorry, matron," said Edward, proceeding towards the staircase.

"What do you want up there?" asked Matron suspiciously.

"It's only a parcel Mr. Ferris asked me to put in his bedroom, matron," said Edward with extreme deference.

"All right, don't dawdle. Good morning, Mrs. Morland. Morland, where's your other hairbrush? I can't only find the one."

"My brush, matron?" asked Tony with interest.

As he looked up in search of further inspiration he saw Edward on the half landing pointing to his pocket in a confidential manner.

"Yes, your hairbrush."

"It's upstairs, matron," said Tony, again deeply grateful to the goddess of truth who so unexpectedly assists the least of her devotees.

"Well, come along now, both of you," said Laura. "We mustn't keep Mr. Knox waiting. I hope I'll see you after tea, matron, and I want to hear all about your leg."

Matron had a historic leg which always became worse at moments of crisis, such as that of the broken window, and to Laura's entirely fictitious interest in it Tony owed a rather privileged position. At the previous half term Laura had found Tony on the verge of serious disgrace for circulating through both dormitories a caricature of matron in her dressing gown with a balloon coming out of her mouth, in which were contained the words, "Shut up or I'll tell the ferret." With the devotion that only a mother's love can inspire, Laura had asked matron to let her see her leg, which she inspected with the deepest attention, bending her head over it with her eyes tight shut. After this matron took a less serious view of the caricature and said that boys would be boys and her married sister's little girl had a wonderful turn for brushwork. The affair blew over without reaching higher quarters and matron became Laura's devoted slave.

In the front seat of the car was George Knox, wearing horn-rimmed spectacles and a large coat with an immense check pattern. Laura had gathered as they drove over from High Rising that since

receiving an offer from an American publisher to do a book on the
Abbots of Barchester he had been dramatizing himself as an American author in search of local color. The little boys hurled themselves
into the back seat and Laura got in beside George Knox.

"Now you can all be quiet," she said as she started the engine. "It's
only ten miles to Barchester, and I may as well drive in peace, because
I know you'll all talk all lunch time. Move your coat a bit, George, it's
all over the machinery."

"I bet your pardon, Laura," said George Knox. "I am indeed
thoughtless, ingrate, to impede or muffle the handles which you so
skillfully manipulate. Figure to yourself, Laura, that in spite of having
had a car for many years, indeed I may say that I was among the
pioneers who blazed the way for that conveyance which is now the
property of the multitude, and a frightful affair that early motor of
mine was, Laura, if you remember it, one which now seems as remote,
as archaic, as the mastodon, in spite, I say of all this, I am still entirely
ignorant of all matters pertaining to it. I see that your car has knobs,
buttons, handles, wires, what do I know? But what do they mean to
me? Nothing."

"That just shows how silly you are," said Laura. "Supposing I
suddenly died at the wheel, what would happen? You would all be
killed because you are too silly to learn to switch off the engine. Tony
could do it, but the car would probably be upside down in a ditch
before he could get at the handle."

"They ought to have an arrangement about that," said Tony,
leaning forward. "They ought to have a dead man's hand like what
they have on the Underground. Have you heard of the dead man's
hand, sir? The driver has to be touching something in his driving
place, and if he falls down dead and isn't touching it, the current gets
cut off and the train stops. It's a jolly good idea, isn't it? And there is
automatic signaling to all the other trains so that they don't all come
up and bump into each other. If they had the dead man's hand on
motors it would stop a lot of accidents. I can show you how to switch
off the engine, sir, it's as easy as anything. Even a baby could do it if it
had any sense. It's like this——"

Tony began to wriggle his whole body over the back of the seat between his mother and George Knox. George Knox pushed him back with a large elbow, while Laura said, "Shut up, Tony, and sit down. And, George, be quiet. You all distract me with your dead men's hands."

George Knox settled himself sulkily in his corner as far as possible from Laura, who took no notice at all. The little boys conducted a monologue about safety devices on railways till they stopped outside the White Hart at Barchester.

Laura led her party into the dining room and chose a table near the window, so that the little boys, who were simmering with excitement at having lunch in an hotel, could look out and see what was happening. The tablecloth, though perfectly clean, appeared to consist entirely of ironmold, and on the table was one of those massive cruets with receptacles for more condiments than a degenerate age can name or furnish.

"And now," said George Knox, taking off his check coat, "what shall we drink?"

"Do take off those ridiculous glasses, George, which you don't in the least need," said Laura, "and then we shall all look less conspicuous. We shall all have oxtail soup and cold veal and ham pie with peas and potatoes, and then you can all say whether you would like pudding, or cheese, or both. The boys will have ginger beer, and I shall have ginger beer with beer in it, and I advise you to have the same, George."

"My dear Laura," said George Knox, who certainly looked more human without his glasses, "matriarch is a term which I should hesitate, on account of our long and tried friendship, though why tried, heaven alone knows, as nothing has ever occurred to try it, to apply to you, but of all the bullying, masterful women I ever knew, not even excepting my mother, who, by the way, writes to me, and this will interest you, Laura, that she has got that secretary of mine, Miss Grey, who gave us all so much trouble last year, as a companion, God help them both, I say, you are undoubtedly the most so. This is not perhaps the exact form in which I should have chosen to couch what

I had it in my mind to say," said George Knox, who appeared to be conscious that his peroration was decidedly weak, "but with you, Laura, a word is as good as a blow, if I make myself clear. What I had originally intended to say, before my mother and Miss Grey intruded themselves unasked into the conversation, which indeed is so entirely typical of both of them, was—what was it, Laura? What the dickens was it?"

"Four bottles of ginger beer and two bottles of beer," said Laura to the waiter, "and some rolls and butter, and bring the lunch as soon as you can. Really, George, I can't be expected to remember what you were going to say when you don't know what it is yourself, and probably never did, but this is very interesting about Miss Grey. She was a very nice girl when she wasn't being a trial, and I expect she and your mother will get on very nicely. Tony, if you can't eat your soup without spilling it you will have to tuck your napkin into your neck."

"But, mother, it's the spoon. Mother, how can people eat soup with a round spoon?"

"Not easily, but it can be done. What part of the cathedral do you specially want to see, George?"

"That, my dear Laura, is immaterial to me."

"In that case, why go at all?" said Laura coldly, but George Knox looked so hurt that she continued, "We'll go up the tower and see the bells. The boys will like it."

"Oh, good on you, mother," said Tony, dropping his spoon clatteringly into his plate. "I know an awful lot about bells, mother. If you have about eight bells you can ring them about forty thousand times. That's permutations and combinations. Do you know about permutations and combinations, sir? It's multiplying all the numbers by each other till you get a perfectly huge amount. Do you know the story of the nails in the horse's shoes, sir? That's permutations and combinations. A man wanted to buy a horse, and so they said how much it was, but he said it was too much, so they said all right, he could pay them a farthing for the first nail in its shoes and a half penny for the second, and so on, always twice as much as the last time and—"

"Be quiet, boy," said George Knox in a loud voice.

"Be quiet, Tony, and eat your veal and ham pie," said Laura at the same moment.

"There is," said George Knox, talking over Laura's gentler voice, "in the book of the Preacher, better known perhaps as the book of Ecclesiastes, a sentence which occurs to me very forcibly at this moment as being not without relevance to the remarks we have just heard. It runs, if my memory serves me rightly—if I do not mistake, it is somewhat as follows—correct me, Laura, if I am inaccurate in any particular—for what is memory but a trick, a convolution of that weak thing the human brain, an association of ideas, a gift from the gods to sear us with regrets for the past or to enable us to revive again the happiness of days that are gone——"

"I can tell you a jolly good way to improve your memory, sir," said Tony, nearly choking himself on a huge mouthful of pie in his anxiety to be helpful to George Knox. "You think of a word and then you think of a word that that word reminds you of, and then you think what that reminds you of, and so on for about twenty words. Then you think what it was that reminded you of the last word and so on right back to the beginning again. For instance, supposing I thought of the word pie, what do you suppose I'd think of next?"

"Printers," said George Knox, hypnotized by Tony's tutorial manner.

"Shepherds," said Laura.

"Flies," said Tony, "and so would Donk. Wouldn't you, Donk?"

Master Wesendonck nodded.

"Why flies?" asked Laura.

"Because we had shepherd's pie last week and I had a dead fly on my plate, so the Ferret gave us all a hundred lines."

"That, my boy, seems an excessive and illogical action," said George Knox with judicial interest. "Why should the presence of a fly, however dead, imply pains and penalties?"

"Well, sir, I put the fly on Donk's plate, and Donk put it on Fairweather's plate, and Fairweather pretended to eat it and then he pretended to be sick, so we all pretended to be sick, so the Ferret went off pop. I should think one would be sick if one did eat dead flies, wouldn't one, sir? Flies have a kind of deleetrious effect on people."

"Deleterious is perhaps the more usual form," said George Knox.

"I know. And so the Ferret gave us each a hundred lines, and he forgot to ask for them, so I and Donk and Fairy have each a hundred lines written out and we are saving them up for when we need them. It's a funny thing about lines—"

"I have it, Laura," said George Knox suddenly. "What Solomon in his wisdom said was: Surely the serpent will bite without enchantment; and a babbler is no better."

"Absolutely perfect, George," said Laura, looking at George Knox with great admiration. "Waiter! Cheese for everyone, please, and a liquor brandy for this gentleman."

"Mr. Knox," said Tony, "do you know what you ought to do if you are bitten by a serpent? You ought to slash the place with a razor blade and suck it and spit out the stuff and rub permanganate in and have strychnine injections and drink a lot of brandy. There aren't many poisonous snakes in England, but the adder can be very dangerous. I dare say you don't know what an adder is like, so I'll tell you."

"Yes, I do know," said George Knox. "And what's more, the babbler is no better. I shall now drink my brandy, hoping, though without much hope, that it may give me some immunity from the human adder. Laura, this meal, poor though it has been, is at my charge."

"Well, George, that's not very politely put when it was my lunch to you, but you can afford it better than I can, so thank you very much. Tony, don't put biscuits in your pocket. It isn't done at hotels."

"But mother, we might find a hungry animal, and you would feel very sad if you met a hungry animal and we had nothing to give it."

"The chances of meeting a hungry animal in the cathedral are so small that we'll risk it," said Laura. "Come along, boys."

The cathedral was only a few minutes' walk from the White Hart. As Laura and her party passed under the arch into the close even Tony and George Knox were faintly conscious of the hushed atmosphere of the place and ceased a rather acrimonious discussion, conducted with confidence and ignorance on both sides, on the nature and effect of antidotes to snake bites. Tony and Master Wesendonck fell behind, while Laura and George Knox strolled on in front, admiring the old brick houses of the close and the greenness of the turf. As they stood waiting in the porch for the boys to come up with them Laura was horrified to see Master Wesendonck draw a mouth organ from his pocket and to hear the strains of "God Save the King," played entirely in thirds, float across the still air.

"Did you know Donk was a mouth organer, mother?" shouted Tony in a loud appreciative voice. "He can play jolly well. He can blow in and out with one breath."

"Don't, don't," said Laura, extremely nervous, as a verger emerged from the swing door. Master Wesendonck had the presence of mind to put his mouth organ in his pocket, while George Knox quickly engaged the verger in conversation about the probable position of the original Saxon church.

The next hour was a nightmare of anxiety and exhaustion for poor Laura. The little boys behaved exquisitely while in the body of the cathedral, but appeared to be under the impression that all corkscrew stairs were outside ecclesiastical jurisdiction and meant for breakneck chases accompanied by loud encouraging calls to one another. Laura, who hated corkscrew stairs and was equally frightened going up or going down, toiled devotedly after them, in expectation of imminent destruction for one or both. At last, worn out, she told the boys to do a final tour of the crypt by themselves and sat down on a seat near the cathedral door to rest. In the nave George Knox and the verger were arguing with determination, and though Laura could not hear what they were talking about she wished they wouldn't, as arguments always frightened her. She closed her eyes for a few moments and retired into her own secret being, which she so rarely had time to visit.

From this meditation she was roused by a sound behind her. Through a low door in a dark corner came Tony and Master Wesendonck, who had finished a most enjoyable tour of the crypt, during which they had both pretended to be ghosts. As they let the door slam behind them with a loud noise that echoed through the whole building Master Wesendonck put his mouth organ to his lips and breathed into it a few solemn chords expressive of the joy of returning from subterranean depths to the light of day. At the same moment George Knox and the verger, still arguing, came round a pillar. With indignant rage the verger strode across to Master Wesendonck and laid his hand on his shoulder.

"Get out of this right away," he almost shouted at the organer, "before I tell the police. I'll tell the dean, and see what he has to say about boys rioting in his cathedral. Out you go, sir, and you too, madam, and the whole boiling of you. I know your school, you boys, and see if I don't tell your teacher of you."

Laura went quite white and felt sick. Any kind of violence always terrified her and she also envisaged Tony's career ruined, or his final apotheosis in a convict's garb, all because Master Wesendonck had played his song of rejoicing on the mouth organ. But George Knox was entirely equal to the occasion.

"Hush, my man," said he to the verger, who looked even more indignant than before at being thus addressed, "remember in whose house you are."

Thus attacked with his own weapons, the ground cut from under his feet, the verger visibly lost courage. George Knox led his party to the exit. As they passed through the swing door he lingered to say to the verger, "Here, my man, is five shillings for your trouble. Your views on the original Saxon church are entirely erroneous, but that is more from ignorance than conviction. And," he added, with a sudden change to a venomous lay voice as he passed the limits of the verger's power, "when you go to see the dean do not omit to give him my visiting card."

He pushed a card and some silver into the verger's hands and walked majestically away.

"Mother," said Tony as George Knox joined them, "don't you think Donk's mouth organ is just like a real organ? When he played those religious chords it was just like a service. Mother, wouldn't it be a good idea if Donk played the mouth organ in church when he comes to stay with us in the summer? It would make a very religious effect. Play a bit of a hymn, Donk."

The sudden fury with which both grown-ups turned on the little boys, commanding instant and permanent silence, was only their reaction from the events of the afternoon. Tony and Master Wesendonck recognized it as such, and with shrugs of the shoulders, silent raisings of the eyes to heaven and other pantomimic gestures, conveyed to each other their opinion of grown-ups who could let such small things affect them. Laura packed her party into the car and drove them all back to the school.

"Such a day, Amy," said Laura to Mrs. Birkett, the headmaster's wife, while the little boys were tidying themselves for tea and Mr. Birkett was showing George Knox, all unwilling, the new cricket pavilion. "George was at the top of his conversational powers and Wesendonck played his mouth organ in the cathedral and the verger was most unpleasant about it. It's fine fun for you to have half term holidays, Amy, and get rid of all the horrible boys, but it isn't any fun for the parents."

She took off her gloves, shoved a few ends of hair under her hat and lay back exhausted in her chair.

"Poor darling," said Amy Birkett kindly. "You shall have tea in a minute and feel better. But it isn't all beer and skittles here either. Matron and Mr. Ferris have had an awful row and aren't on speaking terms, and there is a broken window in one of the cubicles, and matron as good as says that Mr. Ferris broke it himself on purpose, so that one of her boys would get into trouble, and Mr. Ferris says the upper dormitory is a public scandal. I shall be glad when they are all back at work tomorrow."

"Who really broke the window?" asked Laura, whose thoughts unaccountably wandered to her youngest son.

"That we shall probably never know. There is nothing so baffling as the innocence of a guilty boy, except perhaps the guilty appearance of an innocent one. But Edward says the pane had been loose for some time and might easily have been broken if the window was shut rather hard. So we are leaving it at that."

Mr. Birkett now came in with George Knox, and tea arrived, accompanied by Messrs. Morland Jr. and Wesendonck. Conversation was made easy for everyone by George Knox, who embarked on a critical survey of vergers past and present. His review, which included a spirited sketch of the probable characters of the vergers attached to the mysteries of Isis, Mithra, Cybele, Apollo and Baal, with divagations on Ur, Etruria, and the early Christian Church, was powerful and comprehensive, though at times involved. Tony and Master Wesendonck applied themselves to their tea, eating more than seemed humanly possible, while the rest of the company listened to George Knox with glazing eyes.

"So," continued George Knox, "I gave the insufferable fellow my card, and please God, he will show it to the dean. I shared digs with Crawley in my last year at Oxford. Then will the insolent jack-in-office, the base clerical factotum, stew in his own juice, seethe in his mother's milk, though the latter expression, in spite of Biblical precedent, is perhaps out of place. But every cock crows loudest upon his own dung hill — how noble, how resonant, how satisfying, Laura, is the word 'dung,' and how expressive. Thus do vergers strut and exalt themselves in cathedrals, publicans behind their own bars, judges in court, and schoolmasters in their petty province of a few bricks and some dozen of wretched boys."

"Thanks, Knox," said Mr. Birkett. "This seems to me a good moment to leave you, as I have to go and attend to my own petty province."

"Have I given offense?" asked George Knox miserably of Mrs. Birkett.

Mrs. Birkett reassured him.

"Well, Amy," said Laura, "it has been an awful day and thank goodness it's over. Goodbye, Tony darling. Goodbye, Wesendonck. Come along, or we'll be late for dinner."

Laura and Amy went out of the room, while George Knox lingered behind to pass something into the hands of the two little boys. A grateful sigh of "Oh, *thank* you, sir," followed him as he went.

"Believe me, dear Mrs. Birkett," said George Knox earnestly, as he put one leg and half his body into the car, "my sorrow, my contrition, my remorse—no, not remorse, for that is an emotion void of all hope, and most earnestly do I hope to be assured of your forgiveness before I go; with sorrow and contrition, I say, I humble myself before you, craving your indulgent forgetfulness of a slip to which I was led by my wretched tongue. Though I am no talker, no bandier of idle words, my tongue has ever been my bane. A quickness of wit inherited from my Gallic ancestors—"

"Put the rest of your body and your other leg in, George, and shut the door," said Laura.

"—a certain aptitude for seeing the irony of things," said George Knox letting down the window and continuing to address Mrs. Birkett as the car began to move, "these have often led me to say much of which I was afterwards to repent in silence and tears."

By this time the car was halfway down the drive. George Knox turned a large indignant face towards Laura, but as only her profile was visible he was unable to make use of the reproachful gaze he had prepared.

"Not tears, George," said Laura; "and I very much doubt about the silence. Surely the serpent will bite without enchantment."

Tony and Master Wesendonck, their souls full of holy awe at the tip of five shillings each which had just been given them, went to the prep. room and reluctantly got out their books to finish the work which should have been done two days ago.

"You were an ass to be asleep this morning," whispered Tony to Master Wesendonck behind the lid of his desk. "Fairy tried to wake you up, but you wouldn't. We had a splendid time and I swapped some China stamps for some Belgium ones, and my hairbrush and my bedroom slipper got out of the window, and the Ferret came sneaking around, but he never found out who did it. What are you doing?"

Without answering Master Wesendonck pushed across to Tony the Ovid on which he was supposed to be at work. He had been occupying the otherwise profitless hours of preparation by adding mustaches, horns and a tail to the gods and goddesses in the illustrations, and the result, according to prep. room standards, was witty in the extreme. A good deal of latitude was allowed on the evening of a holiday, but the scuffling and giggling that ensued were so distracting as to attract the unfavorable attention of Mr. Prothero, who was taking prep. by reading an Edgar Wallace and did not like being disturbed.

"Morland and Wesendonck, what are you doing?" he asked.

"Nothing, sir," said Tony.

"Nothing, eh?"

"Well, Ovid, sir."

"Well, shut up, both of you, and take a hundred lines," said Mr. Prothero, and plunged once more into the book.

From the mess of papers, books, string, screws, electric wire and dirty handkerchiefs with which his desk was stuffed, Tony extracted a neat copy of a hundred lines and held it up for Master Wesendonck to see. Master Wesendonck nodded in comprehension, and rummaging in his desk, produced in his turn a similar copy. The only alloy in their satisfaction was that Fairweather, not being involved in this particular row, would still have for use on some future occasion the hundred lines which he too had written out for Mr. Ferris and never had to give in. Even so, the thought of having scored a point in the eternal game of Boys v. Masters was so pleasant that they sat with smug contented faces all through prep. till Mr. Prothero, who knew well that something was wrong but couldn't put a name to it, was driven to such a pitch of irritation that he would have willingly given a week's salary to be allowed to thrash them both within an inch of their lives.

III

THE SUMMER HOLIDAYS

CHAPTER I

THE COMPLETE OARSMEN

One hot Saturday in August Tony and his friend, Master Wesen-donck, were to be seen at the gate at the end of the little drive in the uttermost dejection. Master Wesendonck had arrived on the previous day to spend a fortnight of the holidays with Tony, and today was to have been celebrated by a visit to Lord Stoke at Rising Castle, where there was a real ruin and a dungeon. But misfortunes had come thick and fast. Lord Stoke had rung up to say that he had suddenly to go to town, and Tony's mother had fallen a prey to one of her rare and devastating headaches. Tony and Master Wesendonck had then planned to spend the afternoon in the playroom, improving Tony's present railway system and lightening their labors by an occasional tune on Master Wesendonck's mouth organ, but Stoker had thwarted them in these peaceful and reasonable aspirations.

"I dare say you *would* like to play the mouth organ with your poor mother laying there with the headache. Out you both go," said Stoker, "and keep right away from the drawing-room window. You don't want no playing indoors on a nice fine day like this. There'll be something nice for your lunches, and I don't want to see nor hear nothing of you till then. Run along now."

"Run along!" said Tony bitterly, as he and Master Wesendonck strolled up the drive towards the road. "As if we were kids! If I had a bike I'd take you for a ride on the handle bars, but mother won't get me one. She did nearly get me one last Easter, but it had defective steel and got broken, and I would have been killed if I hadn't got off. I expect the chaps at school would have had a half holiday if I'd been killed. Let's sit on the gate and see the motor-bus go past."

Accordingly Master Wesendonck climbed on to the gatepost and there played popular melodies on his mouth organ, while Tony swung to and fro on the gate, as he had often been forbidden to do. The motor-bus went past on its morning journey to Southbridge and the driver waved to Tony. Then it vanished, leaving a cloud of dust behind it, and Tony relapsed into black depression, which even Master Wesendonck's music did little to lighten.

A car came round the corner and drew up at the entrance to the drive. On recognizing his mother's publisher, Adrian Coates, Tony got slowly down.

"Hullo, sir," he said mournfully, "do you want the gate holding open?"

"Yes, please," said Adrian.

Tony opened the gate and Adrian drove through.

"Is that your friend that was here last year when I took you to the Railway Exhibition?" asked Adrian, looking at the musician, who was still perched on the gatepost.

"Yes, sir, that's old Donk. Come on, Donk, we'll have a ride to the house."

"The two little boys attached themselves to the running board. When they got to the front door Stoker came out.

"Can I come to lunch, do you think, Stoker?" asked Adrian.

"There's no one to stop you," said Stoker, with whom Adrian was a considerable favorite. "Mrs. Morland's lying down with the headache. Where's Miss Sibyl and the baby? Mrs. Coates, I suppose I should say, but I can't rightly get used to poor Miss Sibyl being married and having a baby and all. Well, one trouble's enough at a time, and so she'll find."

"They are coming down later by train," said Adrian. "I rather wanted to see Mrs. Morland, but perhaps I'd better not come in if she isn't well."

"Do her good to see a gentleman," said Stoker. "We don't seem to see so much of you since you and Miss Sibyl was married. I hear you've called the baby after Mrs. Morland. I couldn't fancy having a baby called Laura myself. There's a nice bit of steak for lunch and I'll do some more chips."

"Bless you, Stoker," said Adrian, entering the house.

Stoker ushered him into a darkened drawing-room where Laura was lying on the sofa.

"Do you mind if I come in, Laura dear?" asked Adrian. "I didn't want to, but Stoker said it would be all right."

"So long as you don't play a mouth organ I don't care what you do," said Laura feebly. "Have some lunch with the boys. It's very kind of me to offer you any, as it's all your fault that I am lying here like a corpse. You bully me to get books finished for you and then you are surprised that I have headaches."

This unreasonable statement provoked Adrian to retort that it was probably reading thrillers in bed every night that gave his hostess headaches, but the stony silence that followed on his remark made him feel that he had gone too far.

"I'm sorry, Laura," he said. "Would you like me to sit with you or hold your hand or anything? I'll promise not to talk business."

"I would not," said the corpse with surprising vehemence. "If you want to be some use in the world take those boys away for the afternoon—anywhere. Go away."

Adrian tiptoed out of the room and was pounced on by the two little boys, who, with a fiendish pantomime of gnashing teeth, dragged him into the dining-room.

"Where shall we go this afternoon?" asked Adrian as they sat at lunch. "Do you want to see a cinema?"

Master Wesendonck appeared to be about to speak, when Tony burst in.

"Oh, Mr. Coates, could we go on the canal? Donk hasn't ever been on one. We can get awfully good rowing boats and I am pretty decent at rowing. I've been on the Serpentine several times and once on the Thames. The Serpentine really isn't big enough to get a good style. I ought to practice on the Thames. I shall take up rowing when I'm older."

"Can you both swim?" asked Adrian.

"Oh, sir!" cried Tony reproachfully.

The canal, which had once been a highway between two large towns, was now abandoned, except for occasional pleasure parties in the summer. Long stretches of it were choked with weeds, and the towing path was in many places overgrown with grass and brambles, but it was all the more romantic in its derelict condition. About a mile from High Rising there was a little boatshed where boats could be hired during the summer months. The boats belonged to Mr. Brown of the garage and were looked after by his cousin, Henry Brown, whose bicycle Laura had hired for Tony at Easter with such disastrous results.

"Hullo, Henry," said Tony, getting out of Adrian's car with a lordly air, "have you got a decent boat for us?"

"There's the *Annie* and the *Water Lily*," said Henry. "You'd better have the *Water Lily*. The *Annie's* just been painted and she's not quite dry."

The *Water Lily* was a large, comfortable family boat with an ornamental iron railing around the capacious steering seat and two pairs of hybrids which were a cross between sculls and the oars of a ship's dinghy. But niceties of style of nomenclature did not trouble Henry or the customers that used his boats. As all the other boats were out the *Water Lily* it had to be. Henry threw some cushions into her and held her against the bank while the party got in.

"I expect I'd better row first," said Tony, "in case you are tired. I'm pretty good at getting her along. You can steer, sir, but you won't need to steer very much, as I keep a pretty straight course."

Adrian accordingly took his place on the cushioned seat. Master Wesendonck had already climbed silently into the boat and established himself on the prow with his mouth organ.

"Hang on a sec, Henry," said Tony, "while I turn my socks down."

As Tony had bare legs and gym shoes, Adrian wondered what he meant, but Tony drew from his blazer pocket a dirty pair of white socks, took off the gym shoes which he was wearing, put on the socks, put on the shoes again, and rolled the socks down over his shoes.

"It looks better," he said complacently, and stepping heavily into the boat, sat down on the plank seat.

"All right, Henry, let her go," he shouted, taking his blazer off and folding it into a neat parcel. Master Wesendonck blew a blast on the mouth organ, Henry shoved them off with the boat hook, and Tony began to wrestle with the oars. Owing to the capacious nature of the boat, which was of no known class, unless "family" is a recognized make, it was difficult for a little boy to get the oars into the rowlocks, which were farther apart than any that Adrian had ever seen. After some complicated evolutions Tony hit himself in the chest with the end of one oar and fell backwards off his seat.

"Hadn't turned my shirt sleeves up," he explained as he regained his position, as if this would account for all difficulties. "The worst of these boats is they don't have sliding seats. I'm so used to sliding seats that I can't manage so well on a fixed one. Of course, no one who knows anything about boats would ever use anything but a sliding seat."

While he was speaking he had managed to get the oars into the rowlocks and began to row; sometimes in a curious circular way, the oars dipping as far into the water as they rose high above it, sometimes feathering with such intensity that he almost knocked himself off the seat again. As the boat, for all his valiant efforts, made very little progress, Adrian found steering almost useless, and contented himself with shoving the boat away from the bank with a spare oar whenever a collision seemed imminent. Master Wesendonck, who appeared to be of a philosophic turn of mind, devoted himself to his mouth organ and to avoiding being thrown into the water by Tony's erratic course. After one unusually violent bump he stopped playing and took from his pocket a long piece of string. This he tied around one end of his mouth organ, looping the rest around his waist. Having thus insured against the loss of his precious instrument he continued his solitary melodies.

"Doesn't your friend ever play any tunes?" asked Adrian, after some ten minutes of Master Wesendonck's musical arabesques.

"Oh, sir!" Donk has been playing tunes all the time. He is awfully good. In fact he is about the champion mouth organer at school. He got three mouth organs confiscated last term for playing them in the dormitory. Didn't you, Donk?"

Master Wesendonck turned an appraising gaze on his friend and nodded distantly, as if to intimate that he would not be disturbed.

"Would you like your turn now, sir?" asked Tony.

As he spoke he shipped one oar with an effect of careless ease and let the other fall into the water. Adrian collected it as it floated past and exchanged places with Tony. Tony tied his blazer around his neck by the arms and settled himself in the steering seat, sitting well forward, taut and aloof, prepared to contest every inch of the course with an imaginary rival crew.

"Oh, sir," he said reproachfully, as Adrian began to pull the boat out from the bank to which it had drifted, "don't you want to take your coat off? You can't really row properly in a coat. Didn't you notice that I took my coat off?"

"I don't think I am working hard enough, Tony."

"I know. But people might laugh at you if they saw you rowing in your coat. You wouldn't like that, would you, sir?"

At that moment an even larger boat of the family class drew in sight, containing six or seven people rowed by two young men who had very wide views on the art of oarsmanship. Adrian let the *Water Lily* drift near the bank to give them every facility for passing. Tony assumed the expression of the Dauphin in the Temple. Master Wesendonck alone was equal to the occasion, and performed on his instrument several fantasias which evidently expressed pleasure at meeting the new-comers and a wish for their voyage to be successful. Friendly hoots and yells, expressive of the same emotions, came echoing over the water from the other boat as it receded down the long tree-shadowed reach of the canal.

Tony looked at Adrian as equal to equal and shrugged his shoulders.

"Simply rotten," he said. "Did you see them, sir? No style at all. They ought to get someone to tell them how to row. They don't seem even to know how to put their backs into it. You'd be jolly good, sir, if you put a bit more swing into it."

"Thank you," said Adrian, whose repute as an oarsman was not inconsiderable.

"Of course, you can't do much with your coat on," Tony continued. "If you took it off you'd do jolly well. I'd take care of it for you."

Though it was a hot afternoon, the shade on the canal was so pleasant and Adrian had been exerting himself so little, that it had hardly seemed worth while to take his coat off. However, to placate his kind critic he took it off and threw it to Tony, who immediately tied it around his neck by the arms, over his own blazer, and resumed the attitude of the cox of a racing eight. From this position he favored Adrian with a long critical résumé of the styles of the university crews in that year's boat race, from which examination no single member of the dark or light blue crew emerged unscathed. The general impression left on Adrian, who was not listening very attentively, was that until Tony could find leisure to act as cox and crew to both boats the University Boat Race would not be worth seeing.

"Let's get out for a bit," said Adrian after a time. "You and your friend can paddle, Tony. I'm going to sleep."

Accordingly he pulled into the bank opposite the towing path and fastened the boat to an ash sapling.

"Can we bathe?" asked Tony.

"Certainly not."

"Oh, but, sir, we can swim."

"I dare say. But the canal is full of weeds and mud, and your mother didn't say you might bathe, and it's much too hot for me to rescue you. Chuck the cushions out."

Adrian climbed the grassy bank and settled himself on top, under an oak. The August sun was drowsily hot. Adrian, lying on the boat cushions in the shade, thought lazily of poor Laura at home with a headache and felt a vague glow of satisfaction that he was at least relieving her of the boys for the afternoon. Then he thought of his wife and the baby. If it hadn't been for Laura's fostering care he would probably not have acquired a wife and consequently not a baby, and he felt a good deal of gratitude to Laura, combined with very real affection and occasional exasperation. Lulled by such hazily pleasant thoughts, by the sound of bees, by the muffled notes of Master Wesendonck's mouth organ somewhere down by the water's edge, and the far off hum of a reaper and binder, he slipped easily into slumber.

His was no rude awakening. What did penetrate his blissful un-consciousness was an ominous quality of silence. Master Wesendonck's mouth organ was mute; so was Tony's tongue. He yelled once or twice, without much hope of a response, and then with an inward curse on the race of boys he picked up the cushions and went down to the boat, which lay there empty, jackets and shoes thrown about in confusion. Again he called, but no answer came. Thoroughly an-noyed, he threw the cushions into the boat and pulled out into the canal. Behind him lay a long straight reach with overarching trees mirrored in its calm, green water. Before him the canal was hidden by a slight curve a couple of hundred yards away, and a large clump of trees and bushes which came down over the water. Towards this he made his way, less in anxiety than irritation, but any anxiety he may have felt was shortly soothed by a voice from behind the bushes.

"Chuck me over some more of your mud," it said. "We want to bank my side up so that it makes a real harbor."

A few more strokes brought him under the overhanging boughs of a willow and into full view of his young charges. They had strolled along the canal till they found a little bank of mud and stones, and were busily making a small artificial harbor for possible battleships. Both boys were up to their ankles in rich stinking mud, from which lazy bubbles rose at intervals to the surface, exploding in a noisome way. Master Wesendonck, under Tony's directions, was scooping out a channel, while Tony built up a mole. Master Wesendonck's shirt was spotted like a leopard from the spatterings of his dredging activities, while Tony had stripes like a tiger all over his face and arms.

"Stop making that mess," shouted Adrian, "and come on. We've got to get back for tea."

"Oh, sir, must we?" said Tony. "We've nearly finished the harbor. Oh, all right then. Come on, Donk. Of course, we shall never get another chance to finish the harbor, so if all the Morland fleet comes here in a storm and can't find anywhere to anchor, of course they'll simply all be wrecked. We were building a harbor for my battleships, the Morland fleet, sir, and you simply can't have battleships without a harbor for them to go to. How many ships do you think I have now, sir? Twenty dreadnoughts and a hundred cruisers and any amount of T.B.D.s. Do you know what guns my dreadnoughts carry?"

"Did you hear me tell you to come on?" asked Adrian, pulling the boat a few yards on, to where the mud stopped. The little boys came along the bank and were just about to get in, when Adrian, unkindly calling them wart hogs, told them to wash the mud off first. With incredible slowness, taking no apparent notice of Adrian's repeated injunctions to hurry up, they wearily smeared canal water on their filthy arms and legs, Tony keeping up a muttered commentary on the action of people who prevented other people building harbors for their fleets. At last their kind guardian, despairing of any improvement in their appearance, told them to get in as they were. Master Wesendonck again took up his misanthropic position in the bows, and Tony, sinking languidly into the steering seat, began to tie his blazer around his neck again.

"Look here, don't put my coat near your horrible muddy self," said Adrian.

"But, sir, one must have something around one's neck if one is steering, else one catches cold."

"Well, if you touch my coat I'll kill you," said Adrian, who from a glance at his watch knew that Laura would be already wondering which of them was drowned and arranging their funeral. Not that she would care if I were drowned, he reflected almost bitterly, only if it was one of those young mudlarks.

The homeward journey was swift and uneventful. Master Wesen-donck communed with Euterpe in his solitary way, while Tony gave Adrian a few useful hints about his style.

"I expect I'd make an awfully good coach," he said. "I don't know how it is, but I seem to have an instinct about rowing. I seem to give confidence to people. I've given quite a lot of the chaps good advice. I bet I could row as fast as anyone if I had a proper boat with a sliding seat. I bet I could win the Diamond Sculls. Did you ever win the Diamond Sculls, Mr. Coates?"

"No, but I never went in for sculling," said Adrian, finding himself to his horror infected by Tony's boastfulness. "Even if I had, I don't suppose I could have won them," he added by way of penance. "You have to be quite extraordinarily good."

"I know. But if I practiced I dare say I'd get pretty good. My muscles are terrific," added Tony, stretching out one arm suddenly and thereby running the boat right across the canal into the opposite bank.

"Put those ropes down and sit still," said Adrian with an unloving look.

Tony obeyed with cheerful want of interest. Another moment brought them to the boat shed. Here Adrian disembarked, leaving the little boys to collect the jackets and shoes and other loose property in the boat. When he had paid Henry Brown for the hire of the boat he got into his car.

"Hurry up," he shouted to the little boys who were putting their gym shoes on with as much apparent difficulty as if they were savages who had been introduced to footwear for the first time. They rose unwillingly and sauntered towards him.

"Did you bring my coat?" he called to Tony.

Tony turned back, reproach visible in every line of his figure, and got into the *Water Lily*, which was now moored up against the *Annie*.

"Keep away from that paint, you idiot," shouted Adrian. But it was too late. Tony, picking up Adrian's coat in a languid grasp, trailed it across the *Annie's* bows and was trailing it across the grass. Adrian sprang out of the car and snatched the coat from Tony. Luckily the

Annie was almost dry, but there was a smear of brown varnish across one sleeve. He pointed it out to Tony with cold rage.

"I know," said Tony. "If people will leave boats about when the paint isn't dry, it isn't one's fault if paint gets on things. If I painted a boat I'd put it in a place to dry where it wouldn't come off on anything. I'd have a special hot air machine to dry the paint and ——"

But Adrian pushed him into the car with all the annoyance which a brown paint mark on one's new grey flannel suit can produce and drove back to High Rising, where they found Laura at the tea-table.

"I am much better," she announced impressively. "Tell me, did you all have a nice time?"

"Rather," said Tony. "Mr. Coates was awfully decent, mother, and took us on the canal and I rowed quite a lot of the way. My style is pretty good now, but most of the other people we saw had simply rotten styles. I must have a kind of instinct about how to row, haven't I, Mr. Coates? It's partly because my muscles are so good. I bet my muscles are harder than any other chap's in the lower school. There is a chap who has a brother in India, and he has such good muscles that he can let you tie him up with ropes as tight as you like and then burst the rope with one effort of his muscles. I expect my muscles will be like that when I am grown up."

"Did you enjoy it too, Robert?" asked Laura.

Master Wesendonck, whose Christian name appears unexpectedly for the first time, was just going to speak, when Tony, withdrawing from his mouth the large piece of cake that he was about to put into it, answered for his friend.

"Donk had a splendid time. He played his mouth organ like anything. I am pretty good at mouth organing, but Donk has a kind of instinct that I haven't got. Mr. Coates liked his mouth organ, didn't you, sir? I didn't let Donk row, because his style isn't quite trained yet, but he'll be pretty decent when he has had some more practice," he added, flinging his arm around Master Wesendonck's neck.

"Don't skirmish at table," said his mother severely, "or do I mean scrimmage?"

"Mother, I wasn't scrimmaging. Mother, I was only showing affection to old Donk. Mother, if I was all alone in Donk's house and he showed affection to me, you wouldn't call it scrimmaging, would you? Mr. Coates, can I and Donk come and see Sibyl and your baby soon? Has it got any sense yet?"

"Not much," said Adrian, "but Sibyl thinks it has."

"My dear Adrian," said Laura, suddenly up in arms for the honor of her sex, "you are far worse than Sibyl. She is proud of the baby, and quite right too. You pretend you aren't proud just out of pride. It's all inverted something-or-other. Sentiment is your second name," she added severely.

Adrian, remembering the eventful evening on which he had proposed to Laura without meaning to, and her firm handling of him on that occasion, had the grace to look ashamed.

"'I know,' as your son would say, Laura," he answered. "You are quite right as usual. Will you all come to tea tomorrow? Sibyl and her father would love to see you."

Laura said they would all come, and Adrian shortly afterwards took his leave.

"I hope you both behaved well," said Laura when Adrian had gone.

"Of course we did, mother. Of course, if people don't put their boats in safe places when the paint is wet, you can't be surprised at people getting paint on their coats."

"Don't tell me you have paint on you, Tony, as well as all that mud."

"Of course not, mother. Mr. Coates got paint on his coat. Mr. Coates rows jolly well, mother, but I bet my muscles will be bigger than his when I am grown up, and of course he needs a bit more swing in his style, doesn't he, Donk?"

Master Wesendonck blew a blast of acquiescence on the mouth organ, as the two little boys went off to resume work on the railway.

CHAPTER 2

THE NURSERYMAIDS

George Knox, the celebrated biographer, was sitting in his garden at Low Rising with his nice second wife, Anne, and his son-in-law, Adrian Coates. His daughter Sibyl, Adrian's wife, was resting upstairs, and Miss Laura Coates, aged eight weeks and three days, was lying on her back in half a Japanese dress basket. In the dress basket portions of Miss Coates' voluminous luggage had traveled to Low Rising, the upper half swelled well above its natural bounds by its bulky contents, and the whole held together by a couple of stout straps. On arrival one half became Miss Coates' toilet table, while the other half became a temporary bed, in which its owner could be laid in the living rooms or the garden. Miss Coates, lightly clad owing to the heat, was fiercely and determinedly asleep, her arms thrown up on the pillow, though owing to her tender years her arms were so short that they were not within inches of meeting above her head. The pillow was damp with the violence of her slumber. Such hair as she had, which grew ungracefully in a short dark fringe round the back of her head, was also moist with the exertion of being asleep.

The monthly nurse, a delightful young woman called Nurse Chiffinch, was seated starchily in a deck chair, crocheting a mauve bed jacket. Such was her tact that she always sat far enough from her employers to make conversation difficult, though near enough to make it impossible for them to talk privately. As all her friends, so the Coates family gathered, called her Chiffy, her Christian name was unknown, and Adrian was already feeling nervous at the thought of having to ask her when he wrote out her check. For the uncomfortable three or four days when she was in the house before what she called The Event, Adrian and Sibyl had hated her with a hatred that included all the nurses, matrons, probationers and doctors with whom she had ever worked, and about whom she had such an inexhaustible flow of anecdote. From the moment when The Event was imminent she became their best friend and most delightful companion. Her conversation, which, when not professional, was about the royal family, the Tate Gallery, and the various railway stations which her duties had caused her to visit, seemed of absorbing interest to Sibyl as she lay in bed, while Adrian did not dine more than three nights a week at his club.

"What time did you say Laura was coming?" asked Mrs. Knox of her step-son-in-law.

"She didn't say. About tea time, I expect. Tony and his friend with the peculiar name are coming. I have never heard that boy utter yet."

"I don't suppose Tony gives him much chance," said Anne Knox.

"Chance?" said George Knox in his loud emphatic voice. "Good God, Anne, that boy is like Prince Giglio. He could address an army for three days and three nights without the faintest difficulty, on any subject. Did I tell you, Coates, how he met my publisher, Johns, here one day?"

"No," said Adrian, "but I met Johns at a lunch not long afterwards and he was still weak from the effects. He said he had never been given so much advice about the publishing trade in his life. I rather gathered that Tony had offered to go into partnership with him and show him how the business ought to be run."

"How Laura, most admirable of women, in which phrase I do not include my wife, for she is apart, a precious jewel by herself, though undoubtedly a woman too—how Laura, to whom after all in a way I owe the great happiness of my declining years," said George Knox who was about fifty-five and uncommonly healthy, "in that she sheltered my dear wife on that terrible night when her mother, a most trying old lady, Coates, as you probably remember, was removed by death's kindly care, and poor Anne did not know where to turn, and Laura, by suggesting that Lord Stoke would take Anne as a secretary, opened my eyes to the fact that Anne's place was by the dying embers of my hearth, bless them both, I mean Anne and Laura—how Laura, I say again, could have produced such a fountain of useless information, such as an encyclopedia of unwanted and misleading facts, is past my poor comprehension."

"Baby says, 'Please don't talk so loud, grandpa, or you'll disturb my little nap,'" said Nurse Chiffinch, who appeared to have some miraculous power of interpreting Miss Coates' wishes, as that young person was still doggedly asleep.

"My dear lady," cried George Knox, a good deal more energetically than before, "a thousand pardons. Bitterly do I reproach myself for such gross want of thought, and to my own flesh and blood. Are grandchildren one's own flesh and blood?" he asked anxiously.

"Near enough," said his wife. "But it would take more than that to wake Laura."

"Laura?" exclaimed George Knox, dramatically.

"Your granddaughter, George; Sibyl's child."

"I was bewildered," said George Knox, "by the similarity of names; nay, more than similarity, for is not Laura the same, exactly the same, as Laura? Not Amurath an Amurath succeeds, but Laura Laura. Though of course nothing could be more dissimilar than the two bearers of the name. The one a mere embryo——"

"My daughter is *not* an embryo," said Adrian indignantly, but his father-in-law rolled on remorselessly.

"——the other a tender matron, as beautiful in her autumn and as pure as virgins in their spring."

"That's enough, George," said his wife. "Shakespeare and Thackeray in one breath is more than enough. And here is Laura with the boys."

Laura affectionately greeted her hostess, who had been her secretary and valued friend before she married George Knox.

"This is Tony's friend, Wesendonck, who was staying with us at

Easter last year," she said. "You remember him, Anne. How are you, Adrian? Well, George, I'm delighted to see you as a grandfather."

"Even so," said George Knox impressively.

"Even so? What do you mean by that, George? Where is my namesake? Oh, my precious fool, my divine nincompoop!" cried Laura ecstatically, bending over the Japanese basket. "Isn't she the loveliest baby you ever had, nurse?"

"She's a lovely wee thing," said Nurse Chiffinch, "and not a mite of trouble. Are these your little boys?"

"One is," said Laura, "not the other. Don't make a noise, boys; Sibyl's baby is asleep."

The little boys tiptoed over to look into the basket.

"Not a bad kid," said Tony. "Mrs. Knox, Donk has a baby. Donk has three sisters and the youngest is a baby. The others are just little girls. He knows an awful lot about babies. I know a lot about babies myself, because of Donk's baby, so I can tell you a lot of useful things about Sibyl's baby. I expect I'd make a pretty good nurse."

"Isn't your son a scream?" said Nurse Chiffinch.

Laura smiled back at Nurse, a Judas smile which but poorly concealed her cold disfavor at hearing her son called a scream.

"Well, Tony," said Adrian, "how do you like the baby?"

"I expect you think she's pretty interesting," said Tony pityingly. "I must say, sir, she's more what I'd call a thing than an actual person. I dare say she'll get a bit more developed presently. Has she been vaccinated yet?"

"Not yet. Dr. Ford is going to do her next week."

"Good old Dr. Ford!" said Tony enthusiastically. "Can I see him vaccinate her, Mr. Coates? We were all vaccinated last term at school and some of the chaps were awful funks. I bet she'll be a funk. I didn't feel it a bit. I have a kind of special power of not feeling things. There was a master at school whose brother was vaccinated and the doctor put the wrong stuff in and he died. I bet if a doctor put the wrong stuff into me I wouldn't die. I have a kind of power against germs. I was the only one in our house that didn't get chicken pox last summer, because of my power. Can I see the baby vaccinated, sir?"

Miss Coates now woke up, held her breath till she was red all over her face and head and covered with beads of perspiration, relaxed, and lay happily awake.

"I say, Mr. Coates," said Tony, "your baby is awake now. Does she know she is going to be vaccinated?"

"I shouldn't think so. You can tell her."

"Right oh, sir. You needn't be afraid of being vaccinated, darling," said Tony to Miss Coates in a kind and caressing voice, "it's only like a little pin-prick. I'll let you see my railway if you are good and don't cry."

"She doesn't understand yet," said Nurse Chiffinch. "When she's a big girl she'll love to play with your toys and things, won't you, chicky-wicky?"

Tony's face suddenly became perfectly expressionless, and he walked away from Nurse with some dignity.

"Of *course* she can't understand," he confided to Mrs. Knox, "but it's nice for her to be talked to sensibly. If people say things like chicky-wicky she'll never learn English properly. I shall talk sensibly to her and train her to be educated."

"Thank you, Tony; that will be a great help," said Mrs. Knox. "Now come along in to tea."

Nurse picked up the basket full of baby and carried it off to the house, while the others followed. Tea was at a round table in the cool dining-room, where Sibyl joined them.

"I say, Sibyl," said Tony, as soon as they were seated, "she's a decent baby. I'm going to teach her to talk sense. You oughtn't to teach babies to talk nonsense, it makes them not be educated. If I had a baby, do you know what I'd do?"

"No. What?"

"Do you know, Mr. Knox?" said Tony, raising his voice.

"Know what, my boy?" said George Knox, startled from a conversation he was having with Laura about his new life of Charles II.

"Don't interrupt, Tony," said his mother.

"But, mother, what do you think I would do if I had a baby? I'd teach it everything in the world while it was too little to mind. It's only when you get older that you mind learning things. When I was quite little I didn't mind learning things a bit, but now I get a kind of exhaustion of learning. It's all this exam system, Mr. Knox. If it wasn't for exams schools would be quite decent. I'm pretty good at exams though. I have a kind of gift for keeping my head in exams. I expect I'll always do pretty well in exams. It's just a kind of power I have."

At this moment Nurse came back.

"I've left baby in the pram, just outside, Mrs. Coates," she said, taking her seat at the table.

"Oh, can I push the pram?" asked Tony. "Donk's baby has a pram, and he pushes it quite a lot. Don't you, Donk?"

"What is that child's name?" asked George Knox.

"Wesendonck," said Laura.

"Mr. Coates, can I push the baby's pram?" said Tony again. "Donk and I could give her lovely rides. We'll make the pram be the down express and go thundering through High Rising and crash over the points at Southbridge till we get to Southampton."

"Certainly not," said Adrian. "You'll leave the perambulator alone, both of you."

"I don't know Southbridge," said Nurse Chiffinch, "but I had to change at Southampton West when I was nursing General Fowkes's wife in the New Forest. The station there is quite a paltry affair."

"I know," said Tony, evidently under the impression that he had discovered a fellow enthusiast, "but you get marvelous trains through Southampton West. You get composite trains from Reading and Bath and Cheltenham and Manchester——"

"Cheltenham is a sweetly pretty place," said Nurse. "I was there with Mrs. Le Poer who was a cousin of the General's. Her husband was in India at the time, but the baby was a bonny wee mite."

"Do you mean the Great Western station or the L.M.S. one?" asked Tony, who had been eagerly waiting to get this question in. "The L.M.S. one is called Lansdown and it's about half a mile from the Great Western one."

"Oh, I couldn't say, I'm sure," said Nurse Chiffinch. "You are quite

a little authority on trains, aren't you? I never heard your name. What
is it?"

"Tony Morland," said the bearer of that name sulkily, disappointed
in the technical talk to which he had been looking forward.

"Is it your mummie that writes the books?" asked Nurse Chiffinch,
with a comprehensive view of all literature. "Well, I never thought I'd
meet two authors. What a lucky little boy you are to have a mummie
writing such lovely books. I get all your books from the library, Mrs.
Morland. I quite revel in them."

Laura, whose first impulse was to distract anyone who professed
open admiration for her books, while she secretly despised people
who didn't, became a prey to schoolgirl embarrassment and was
unable to say anything. Not so her son.

"I expect you are the kind of audience that *would* read mother's
books," he said, studying Nurse with scientific interest. "Her books
are pretty good, but there are long places of dullness. I think the
improbableness makes them interesting sometimes. Donk and I are
going to write a play, aren't we, Donk?"

"Laura, tell me, in pity, once more, what *is* that child's name?" said
George Knox.

"Wesendonck, George."

"I know, I know," cried George, hitting his brow dramatically.

"Don't say 'I know' when I tell you things," said Laura snappishly.
"You are as bad as Tony."

"Far be it from me, dear Laura, to claim omniscience," said George
Knox. "Anne will tell you how frail, how human is my intellect. But I
merely used the expression as one might say 'Thalassa!' because——"

"You can say Thalassa or Thalatta, sir," said Tony. "You couldn't
understand it all if I explained. I dare say you haven't heard about the
digamma and the iota subscript——"

"I know much more about it than you do," roared George Knox,
quite overcome with fury. "I took a first in Greats in nineteen hundred
and three. What I was trying to say, Laura, when that ill-omened
child of yours interrupted me, was that I suddenly remembered the
associations of the name Wesendonck. Wagner's friends. Of course,

of course. Doubtless this child comes from the same stem. How strange are names. Look at us all seated around my tea-table. Not one of us but has a name recalling glories past or present. I myself bear the name, though thank God he is no connection of mine, of Scotland's Great Reformer, probably one of the most disagreeable men who ever existed."

"I know," said Tony. "Mother, can I and Donk go in the garden?"

Laura nodded. The two little boys rose from their chairs, scraping the tablecloth sideways as they did so, knocked a knife on to the floor and left the room.

"My wife," continued George Knox, "and let me say *en parenthèse*, Laura, how thankful I am to see the last, though his absence may be but temporary, of your son, with his inscrutable face and appalling flow of information, bore before marrying me the name of Todd. What does this convey to us?"

"Sweeney Todd," said Laura promptly.

"Right, right, my dear Laura. And now she shares with me the name of Knox, a name which—"

"You've done Knox, George," said Laura, "so we needn't have it all over again. And I am Morland, which reminds you curiously enough of George Morland, who painted pigs, and Wesendonck you've done, and Adrian doesn't count. So now let's go in the garden."

"Stay!" said George Knox.

Everyone stayed.

"I charge myself with gross discourtesy," said George Knox. "There is one among us, one to whom both my daughter, my son-in-law and myself—Anne, why is there not a word in English which means 'both' when it applies to three?"

Sibyl suggested tricycle. Nurse Chiffinch, who had taken the mauve bed jacket from a jade green bag, said that two was company and three was none, as the saying was, but she herself was never so happy as in the company of her pals Wardy and Heathy that she shared the flat with.

"Don't say 'both' at all," said Laura in her deepest voice.

"—one among us, to whom my daughter, my son-in-law and

myself conjointly owe gratitude," said George Knox, swelling with
literary pride at having surmounted this obstacle, "whose name re-
calls, how vividly, the court of the monarch on whose life I am now
engaged. If we think of a backstairs purveyor of beauty for his royal
master, a subtle and conscienceless knave, immortalized by Scott in
'Peveril of the Peak.' though that work in itself is hardly up to the level
of Scott's masterpieces, bearing as it does traces of the strain and
fatigue to which that noble nature was subjected, what is the name
that springs at once to our mind?"

Everyone present, except the owner of the name, who was placidly
doing her crochet, had seen for some time what was coming, but
hypnotized by the approach of danger was unable to make any effort
to stem George's eloquence.

At that moment Annie, the parlormaid, made an opportune appearance. With the skill born of long practice she waited for her
master to take breath, and addressing Laura said if convenient she
would wish to speak to her. In some trepidation, for rarely does a
parlormaid wish to speak of anything but misfortune, Laura rose and
followed Annie from the room. She was prepared to hear that Tony
had drowned himself in the Rising, or put his toes into the lawn
mower, or fallen down the well in the kitchen garden, but she was not
prepared for Annie's next remark.

"I thought you'd like to know, madam, that the young gentlemen
have got the pram," said Annie with pleasurable excitement, "and
Master Tony says it's a steam engine. I hope I did right to tell you."

"Where did they go, Annie?" asked Laura.

"Down the stone path by the river, madam. Master Tony did say
something about the Cornish Express," said Annie giggling.

"Go and tell Nurse to come at once," said Laura, "but don't let
anyone else know."

She hurried down the grass walk. As she turned the corner towards
the river Tony came into view, careering madly along behind the
perambulator and making for the river at full till.

"Come back, Tony," shouted his mother.

"I'm the Cornish Riviera Express, mother," Tony shouted back, either not hearing or ignoring her command. "Watch me go over the Saltash Bridge, mother."

He raced on towards the plank bridge which spanned the little river Rising. Laura began to run, but Tony was well away. With an ear splitting yell, meant to represent the King George V's whistle, he plunged on to the bridge. The planks were narrow, the wheels perilously near the edge. A wheel slipped over and the perambulator became wedged at a slant, only prevented by the rickety handrail from falling into the river. Tony wrestled with it for a moment, shrugged his shoulders, and came back towards his mother.

"Where is the baby?" said Laura, breathless.

"I don't know, mother. Mother, did you see the wreck of the Flying Cornishman?"

Laura's heart stopped beating for an appreciable space of time. She knew that Adrian and Sibyl's baby was either strangled or suffocated in the perambulator, or was lying sodden in the bed of the river Rising, but she could find no strength, no words to shriek out the news.

"The other little boy has got baby quite safe, Mrs. Morland," said Nurse, who had come up behind her, with unabated calm and cheerfulness. "Aren't those boys a scream. Come along, Tommy, and show mummie where the baby is."

Tony looked around with interest for the new arrival.

"It's Tony, not Tommy," said Laura, pulling herself together.

"There now, I thought it was Tommy," said Nurse. "Well, you are a pickle, aren't you, sonny? Give us all a fright like that. I don't know what mummie will do to you."

"Kill him," said his doting parent.

"But, mother," said Tony much aggrieved, "Donk has got Sibyl's baby. Of course, we took her out of the perambulator first. Did you think your son would have so much senselessness?"

"I did."

"Oh, mother! Donk knows all about babies, mother. His mother lets him nurse his baby sister as much as he likes. Mother, if I had a baby sister I could get quite practiced with babies."

"Well, thank heaven you haven't," snapped his mother. "Boys are trouble enough. Come back at once. Poor Sibyl will wonder where the baby is."

Still injured, Tony led the way back to the house. Just outside the dining-room window, on a low garden seat, sat Master Wesendonck, the perambulator rug spread on his knees and Miss Coates lying flat on her back on his lap being adored, with Annie as an interested spectator.

"Hello, Donk," said Tony, "I had a splendid accident with the Cornish Express."

Master Wesendonck nodded distantly at his friend and relapsed into his attitude of brooding admiration.

"Robert, you shouldn't have taken the baby out of the perambulator," said Laura, "you frightened me dreadfully and you might have dropped the baby or hurt her."

Master Wesendonck said nothing, but invited Laura with a glance to look at his hands. Miss Coates held his two little fingers tightly closed in her two fists and appeared to derive considerable enjoyment from the exercise.

"I'd like a snap of them just like that," said Nurse Chiffinch. "Quite a picture they make. Come along now, chicky-wicky, time for beddy-byes."

With a deft movement she scooped up Miss Coates and her rug and carried her away. Tony disappeared towards the stable. Master Wesendonck sat on, rapt, while Laura went in to reassure the family. To her considerable annoyance they were quite undisturbed. Annie, it seemed, had only waited for Laura's hurried rescue expedition to depart to remember to tell Sibyl that the other young gentleman had the baby. Having satisfied herself that her daughter was happy with Master Wesendonck, and left Annie on guard, Sibyl had done all that she thought necessary. Laura, shattered by her experience, took some pleasure in letting the unruffled Sibyl know that the perambulator was a derelict on the plank bridge.

"You will fetch it, won't you, Adrian darling?" said Sibyl.

"Mother," said Tony, when his mother came up to see the little boys in bed that night, "did you see the rug on old Donk's knees when he was taking care of the baby? Do you know why he had the rug on his knees, mother?"

"For the baby to lie on, I suppose."

"Yes, I know, but there was another reason too. Donk thought the baby might be a little lonely without her mother or her nurse, so he put the rug on his knees so that she would think it was Sibyl or the nurse. You see, mother, women have skirts and boys have knickers, so Donk thought that if he put the rug on, the baby would think he was her nurse. You see, the rug made a kind of skirt, mother, so that the baby——"

"You needn't explain it any more, Tony," said Laura, secretly touched. "Did you tell Sibyl you were sorry for being such a nuisance?"

"Oh, mother! I only took the pram to be the Cornish Riviera Express. Donk took heaps of care of the baby. Didn't you, Donk?"

As usual Master Wesendonck remained silent, but there was something different in the quality of his silence which Laura at once felt.

"Is anything wrong?" she asked anxiously.

Master Wesendonck shook his head silently, and rolled over in his bed with his back to his hostess.

"Mother," said Tony, pulling Laura down with urgent hands and whispering, "Donk is a bit homesick for his own baby. He got a bit homesick because of having Sibyl's baby to hold. Poor old Donk. He's a decent chap, mother."

Laura went across to the other bed and bent over it.

"You don't want to go home, do you?" she asked anxiously.

Once more Master Wesendonck shook his head.

"Would you like to go and see the baby again tomorrow?" she asked.

Master Wesendonck sprang to a sitting position, reached out two skinny arms and gave his hostess a violent hug. Then he detached himself, and lying down, apparently went straight to sleep.

"Good old Donk," said Tony.

CHAPTER 3

THE STOKEY HOLE

Lord Stoke was a man of his word. Some grown-ups say they will do a thing, and if you ask them When, they say, Someday. But someday, as Tony very truly remarked, is in the days that never come. Lord Stoke was not a grown-up of this kidney. He had promised Tony a day at Rising Castle and had been obliged to postpone the treat, but two or three days later he rang Laura up and asked her to come to lunch and bring her little boy and anyone she had staying with her. Therefore at breakfast she extended the invitation to Master Wesendonck, who was trying to cut all the white away from a poached egg, leaving the pure yellow center on its piece of toast.

"Oh, mother, good on Lord Stoke," said Tony. "Donk will love to come. Mother, do you see what Donk is doing? He is cutting off all the white of his egg. Then he can put the yolk into his mouth all at once, and it will make the plate not so messy and save Stokes a lot of washing up. Mother, look."

Master Wesendonck had succeeded in freeing the yolk from all white, and was lifting it precariously on his fork, prepared to make a mouthful of it. As Tony spoke the yolk bulged perilously sideways and fell off. By great good luck it landed on the toast, unscathed.

Tony drew a deep breath.

"Mother, did you see?" he said. "Donk's egg wasn't broken. Wasn't

it lucky? He is an awfully lucky chap like that, mother. Once at school
we were having sardines for breakfast and Donk betted one of the
chaps he'd put six in his mouth at once, so he got some extra sardines
from some other chaps and he mashed them all up into a kind of
paste, mother, and then Mr. Prothero said what was he doing, so
Donk said, 'Nothing, sir,' so Mr. Prothero said, 'Get on with your
breakfast.' So Donk put all the paste into his mouth at once, and when
he tried to chew it it all came squeezing out of his mouth and he had
to drink a lot of tea to help him to swallow it."

When this pointless and unpleasant anecdote had come to an end
Laura said coldly: "Why was it lucky, Tony?"

"Oh, mother! He got a lot of extra sardines. Mother, can we go
exploring at Rising Castle?"

"I expect so."

"Oh, good on you, mother. We'll take our torches, won't we,
Donk?"

Master Wesendonck, who had suspended his egg operations to
listen to his friend's saga of his feat with the sardines, was now making
a second attempt to convey the whole yolk to his mouth. This time he
was successful, and all that was left of the egg was an orange border
around his mouth.

"Now both go and wash your faces," said Laura, "and be ready at
ten minutes past one to go to Rising Castle. Tell Stoker to see that you
are respectable. I'm going to write."

"Come on, Donk," said Tony. "As a matter of fact I was just
thinking of washing my face, anyhow."

The morning sped away all too fast for Laura, who was behind-
hand with some more stories about Madame Koska which had been
commissioned by an American magazine. Madame Koska was in
frightful difficulties because her head fitter, on whom much of the
success of her establishment depended, had been mysteriously absent
for two days. As no one knew where she lived—for on these lines did
Madame run her business—her employer had just called in the
police. Laura, who was writing from hand to mouth without any idea
of what was to happen next, could not decide whether the fitter,

known by Madame to be a Russian ex-aristocrat, had been abducted by political enemies, or had merely gone to the nearest bomb factory to join the anarchists. So she sat with pencil poised and her hair wildly disheveled, waiting for inspiration that would not come.

Gradually voices in the garden below her window obtruded themselves upon her consciousness and resolved themselves into the well known tones of Stoker and Tony having a difference of opinion. Finding literary composition impossible, she got up and looked out of the window.

Tony, assisted by Master Wesendonck, was sitting cross-legged on the lawn with a quantity of brown paper and string. Beside him was the dining-room wastepaper basket.

"What are you doing, Master Tony?" asked Stoker, coming out of the front door with a broom in one hand and a duster in the other.

"Nothing," said Tony, without looking up.

"That's easy said," remarked Stoker. "And what's that in the waste-paper basket?"

"Well, Stokes, if we go to Rising Castle we must take something for the peacocks. Suppose you were a peacock, Stokes, and lived in a garden with wretched things like worms and seeds to eat, and some-one came to see you, wouldn't you be very disappointed if they didn't bring some treats for you?"

"There's no sense in saying what I'd do or not do if I was a peacock," said Stoker.

"Because you'd be a peahen," said Tony, at which brilliant riposte Master Wesendonck was heard to laugh.

"Any more of that and I'll tell your mother, Master Tony. Let me see what's in that basket."

In spite of Tony's protests she turned the basket upside down on to a piece of the brown paper. A cascade of lump sugar came rolling out, followed by some biscuits and several pieces of bread.

"Back it all goes where it come from," said Stoker, pointing with the broom towards the house.

"Oh, Stokes, animals need sugar. Haven't you heard of salt-licks?" If animals don't get salt they die, and sugar is just as important."

"Never heard of no sugar-licks," said Stoker.

Here Master Wesendonck was moved to laugh again. Tony looked contemptuously at his friend, who was tying a piece of brown paper on his head with string as if it were a bonnet, and did not notice Tony's withering glance.

"Oh, Stokes, do let me have just some sugar and biscuits."

Stoker, flattered by Master Wesendonck's reception of her joke, began to unbend.

"Well, you can have some sugar and a bit of bread," she said, "but not one of your poor mother's biscuits do you have. There she sits, writing that rubbishy stuff of hers year in year out, just to keep you at school, Master Tony, and we can't afford to buy no biscuits to give to no animals, let alone peacocks."

"I know. I say, Stokes, could I have about three biscuits for the peacocks? They would be so pleased."

As he spoke he arranged a neat pile of the pieces of bread, six biscuits, and about three-quarters of a pound of sugar on a piece of paper, and looked up at Stoker with the angelic blue eyes of a humanitarian.

Stoker, of course, gave in, though for form's sake she carried the remaining four biscuits and a few lumps of sugar back into the house. Laura went back to her work. That admirable woman thought so humbly of her own potboiling that to hear it stigmatized by a critic of Stoker's mental powers as rubbishy stuff didn't depress her in the least. If she could have made it more rubbishy, and so sold more thousands of copies than she did, she would willingly have done so, but the artist in her, on whose existence George Knox and Adrian always insisted, kept her standard up, firmly if spasmodically.

At ten minutes past one the little boys, cleaned within an inch of their lives by Stoker, were ready. Laura brought the car around and called to them to get in. Tony was carrying a large shapeless parcel, ingeniously secured with a network of string, which his mother guessed to be the food for Lord Stoke's pampered peacocks. For a while there was silence as they drove through the village.

"Some people," said Tony to Master Wesendonck and a few other invisible friends, "wouldn't think of prevention of cruelty to animals. I don't know how it is, but I have a great understanding of animals. I know exactly what it feels like to be an animal, so I know what they want. If animals live on grass and things, they need something else for a treat. Mother, did you notice my parcel?"

"I did."

"Well, mother, that is prevention of cruelty to animals. Lord Stoke's peacocks don't get any treats, so I have got a parcel of treats for them."

"I know," said Laura.

This use of his own favorite gambit so stunned her son that she was able to proceed: "I happened to be looking out of the window when Stoker told you not to take all those biscuits and the sugar. Tony, you *must* ask me before you take things from the kitchen."

"I know. People," he added bitterly, but audibly, "don't care if animals don't get any treats. They haven't any instinct for animals. Have they, Donk?"

But Master Wesendonck, who had torn a small hole in the parcel, was making a heavy ante-lunch of sugar and biscuit, so that his mouth was too full to answer. For a moment Tony's face darkened at this attack on the defenseless animal race, but in a forgiving spirit he assisted his friend in sampling the peacocks' treat.

Rising Castle was situated on a hill at the confluence of the Rising and Rushmere Brook. It boasted a Norman keep in fair condition and a good deal of the original walls. The fourth Lord Stoke had defended the castle against Cromwell, who had unpleasantly battered him into honorable capitulation. After several generations of neglect the present earl's great-grandfather had built a comfortable mansion from the stones of the ruins. The present owner had put such parts of the castle as were still standing into tolerable repair and allowed the public to visit them at sixpence a head. There was also a large natural cave below the castle, known locally as the Stokey Hole. It had an opening onto the banks of Rushmere Brook and was popularly supposed to communicate by subterranean passages with Capes Castle, ten miles off, a disused windmill on the hills beyond Southbridge, and the

Tower of London. But this was more a matter of faith than actual experiment.

As they drove up to the door Laura recognized Dr. Ford's two-seater standing in the drive. She was pleased to see it, as it meant that the doctor, a great friend of Lord Stoke, would probably be staying to lunch and would help her to keep her resilient son in his place. They found Lord Stoke, a benevolent and slightly deaf old gentleman with an antiquarian bent, talking to Dr. Ford in the hall, and immediately went in to lunch.

"I have read your last book, Mrs. Morland," said Lord Stoke, who was very fond of Laura. "Delightful, if I may say so. How you keep it up is beyond me."

"Oh, I just go on," said Laura vaguely.

"Mother's last book is jolly good," said Tony. "Of course, a lot of it's dull, but I dare say you wouldn't notice that, sir."

"Shut up," said Dr. Ford.

"I hope you won't put me into a book, Mrs. Morland," said Lord Stoke, who was one of those people who are under the impression that all authors go about studying their friends with a view to copy.

"I couldn't," said Laura. "You would be much too difficult."

Lord Stoke bridled. Dr. Ford caught Laura's eye and knew that they were both having the same thought, namely that any book with Lord Stoke as a principal, or even a subordinate character, would fall dead with its own weight.

"Oh, Dr. Ford, can I see Sibyl's baby vaccinated?" said Tony earnestly. "I'm jolly good at seeing people vaccinated. I saw all the other chaps vaccinated at school last term. I'd like to do some vaccinating myself. I'd have a lot of flimp——"

"Lymph, perhaps you mean," said Dr. Ford.

"I know. I'd have heaps of flimp and simply bung it into their arms. Oh, Dr. Ford, *can* I see the baby vaccinated?" he implored, rocking backwards and forwards in his chair with excitement at the prospect.

"Certainly not."

"Well, then, can we explore Stokey Hole, Lord Stoke?" asked Tony, speaking from an upside down position in which he was rescuing a potato that had somehow got under the table. His host did not hear the question, so Laura repeated it.

"Better not," said Lord Stoke. "Some of the underground passages are very long, and you might get lost. But you can go up the keep and all over the towers. I have had most of the stairs repaired since you were last here, Mrs. Morland."

"Any more theories about Stokey Hole?" asked Dr. Ford.

"I had a man down here the other day who knew the caves of Locmaria in Brittany very well. He thinks there are traces of the same kind of work in each and that they have some ritual significance. But as no one can agree whether Stokey Hole is natural or artificial, that doesn't get one anywhere, besides being highly improbable," said his lordship sadly.

"I'll tell you what you ought to do, sir," said Tony. "You ought to get a lot of string and let people go along the passages with torches."

"Yes?" said Lord Stoke, courteously.

"Well, then, sir, they couldn't get lost, and they might find some clues. I bet if I went down Stokey Hole I'd find some remains— Roman or something. I should know all about Roman remains because I've done Ovid and Livy."

"Too late, my boy," said Dr. Ford. "The caves were explored and mapped about fifteen years ago, and all the remains are in South-bridge Museum. I was there, and I can assure you that there were no Roman remains. Mostly stinking remains of vermin," said Dr. Ford reminiscently.

"I know. Mother, *could* I and Donk go into Stokey Hole this afternoon? I bet we'd discover something."

"Shut up," said Dr. Ford.

Tony's face became expressionless, except for a faint flicker of contempt, and he applied himself to cherry pie. Lord Stoke asked Laura about the George Knoxes in whom he took a neighborly interest. Laura was becoming lyrical on the subject of Adrian and Sibyl's baby, when her eye fell on Tony's plate.

"What have you done with your cherry stones, Tony?" she asked anxiously. "And Robert, where are yours? You haven't swallowed them, have you?"

Neither little boy answered. Silence from Master Wesendonck was so normal as to be unnoticeable, but in Tony it took on a sinister aspect.

"Have you swallowed them, you idiots, or thrown them under the table, or what?" said Laura impatiently.

Tony winked at his friend, and each ejected from his mouth an apparently endless stream of cherry stones, which rolled loudly on to their plates. A young footman laughed and was blighted by the butler.

"I *am* so sorry, Lord Stoke," said poor Laura, angry and confused. "One's children and their friends are born to mortify one."

"But, mother," said Tony, "I betted Donk I'd get more cherry stones into my mouth than he could. How many did you have, Donk?"

Master Wesendonck, busily separating his stones into little heaps of four, made no answer.

"Oh, only twenty-one," said Tony glancing contemptuously at his friend's plate. "I had twenty-eight. Lord Stoke, I had twenty-eight stones in my mouth. Did you see twenty-eight stones coming out of my mouth, Dr. Ford? I saved them all up in my mouth till I had twenty-eight. Mother, did you see Albert laughing?"

"Albert?"

"Yes, mother. You know Albert. He is Mr. Knox's Annie's brother. I winked at him and he winked back."

The butler, who was pouring out port for Dr. Ford, assumed a reserved expression which augured ill for the too friendly Albert.

"You know Albert, of course, sir," said Tony to Lord Stoke, "because he lives here. He can play the mouth organ even better than Donk, and he has a double-jointed thumb. Stoker says it's because his mother had a turn, but Annie says——"

"SHUT UP," said Dr. Ford.

Lord Stoke, handicapped by his deafness, had been vainly wrestling with the problems of why George Knox should have a brother called Albert who appeared to be in the room, though invisible to him, and what it was that he himself had said about someone having a turn, though this he was sure as a misstatement. Laura and Dr. Ford, realizing his confusion and hoping to avoid any further outbreaks from Tony, suggested that their host should show them his latest restoration work on the castle. Dr. Ford lingered behind, letting Lord Stoke go in front with Laura.

"Listen," he said to the boys, "neither of you is to go near Stokey Hole — not even *near* it. Do you hear me, Tony? You are both much more trouble than you are worth, and I am not going to have your mother and Lord Stoke worried. You'll probably fall off the keep and kill yourselves, anyway, but if you do, at least everyone will know where you are. If you go into that hole I shan't be able to keep my eye on you, so you aren't going. Is that clear? Now, come along."

"I know," said Tony. "Dr. Ford, I had twenty-eight stones, so that means I'll never be married. Donk had twenty-one, so he'll be married this year. I bet everyone will laugh if he does. I'd laugh like anything if Donk was married."

Master Wesendonck scowled at his friend and hit out in his direction. Tony closed joyfully with him and the two little boys followed Dr. Ford in a welter of arms and legs.

Lord Stoke, with maddening slowness and infinite wealth of de-tailed explanation of what he and his architect had been doing, then showed them the piece of Norman wall that he was rebuilding, the foundations of what might have been a chapel, and the room in which it was on the whole improbable that Charles II had slept after the battle of Worcester. Laura's thoughts were divided between her host, to whom politeness forced her to give some kind of attention, and her young charges, who raced up and down winding staircases, hung out of crumbling turret windows, walked along insecure ledges, and vanished for ten minutes at a time to reappear on portions of the building marked "Danger. Closed to Visitors."

At last the horrid treat came to an end and Lord Stoke allowed his party to rest on a seat in the inner ward and take breath. The sight of peacocks walking about on the grass below the grey walls reminded Tony of his mission to animals.

"I expect your peacocks don't get many treats, sir," he remarked to Lord Stoke.

"Eh, what, my boy?" said his lordship.

"I said I expected your peacocks didn't get many treats, sir. I expect you are too busy to think about them much. If I was very busy I'd have a special time for thinking about animals. I thought about your peacocks today when I was very busy having my breakfast, and I brought a treat for them. It's in the car. Can I give it to them, sir? It's sugar and biscuits. Animals all need sugar, you know, and they like biscuits, too, so it would be a treat for them to have biscuits and sugar together."

Lord Stoke, who had understood little or nothing of what Tony was saying, seized on the last word.

"Feathers?" he asked kindly. "Well, my boy, I'm afraid they have finished molting, but if you can find any feathers about you are welcome to them. They are unlucky, you know."

"I know," said Tony. "Thank most awfully, sir. Come on, Donk, let's find some feathers and we'll give them to Sibyl's baby."

The little boys dashed off across the grass, leaving their elders in peace.

"Do you mind having peacock's feathers in the house, Mrs. Morland?" asked Lord Stoke.

"Not a bit. I was married on a Friday which was the thirteenth of May and changed the name and not the letter, but I always felt quite equal to having all the back luck I wanted without worrying about feathers," said Laura.

Dr. Ford, who appeared to have disentangled the meaning of her rather involved remarks, looked admiringly at her. Lord Stoke then suggested that they should take a stroll around the river bank outside the castle walls, picking up the little boys on their return. Accordingly they went out by the old water gate, to where a grassy path meandered along the bank above the Rising. At the point where the Rising and Rushmere Brook joined they stopped to admire the view, and then returned on the other side of the castle up the valley of Rushmere Brook. The path at this point lay below a steep rocky bank above

which the castle rose towering. Lord Stoke stopped to show Laura the
cavern halfway up the bank where the Stokey Hole had one of its
exits.

From the mouth of the hole came the sound of an animated, if
one-sided, conversation, punctuated by the strains of a mouth organ,
which caused Laura and Dr. Ford to exchange amused and exasperated glances. From the first words it was evident that the little boys,
disregarding all injunctions, had made their way into the Stokey Hole
and explored some of its ramifications.

"Come on, Donk," said Tony's voice. "Let's go back in the Stokey
Hole and explore. We might get to the Tower of London. Stoker has
a nephew in the Tower of London, and he said he wouldn't be
surprised what happened there. I bet he'd be surprised if he suddenly
saw us coming out of a secret passage. Come on, we've got our
torches."

A defiant blast was heard from Master Wesendonck's mouth
organ.

"Anyway," said Tony, "Dr. Ford only meant he didn't want us to go
into Stokey Hole if he knew we were going. He didn't say not to go if
he didn't know we were going, because then he wouldn't worry.
Anyway, I bet he's never been as far as we did. Come on."

"Tony!" cried his mother, with a peahen screech which made Lord
Stoke jump through all his deafness, and even surprised Dr. Ford,
who knew her very well. "Come down at once."

Tony looked down at his mother with a polite interested face and
waved his hand.

"Come down, I said," she repeated.

"Oh, mother, need we? Mother, we were going exploring."

"Come down at once, both of you," shouted Laura, pale with
apprehension that both little boys would be engulfed in Stokey Hole
and never found again till the rats had gnawed their bones.

"Oh, all right then, mother. If people don't want one to do useful
things like exploring of course it's all no good. Give me the feathers,
Donk."

A hostile silence seemed to indicate that Master Wesendonck was not prepared to accede to his friend's demands.

"All right," said Tony, emerging on to the little mound in front of the hole and turning his back on his friend, "keep them, then. Anyone could tell you that Sibyl's baby is much too young to appreciate feathers, but some people have no sense."

As he spoke he walked scornfully forward on to nothing, clutched at a bush which came away in his grasp, and rolled over and over down the bank till he arrived, all the worse for his journey, at his mother's feet. For a moment he was stunned, more by the surprise than by the actual fall. His face went very pink, and as he picked himself up with battered knees and a small cut on his forehead his eyes looked suspiciously wet.

"It all comes of hideous, deliberate disobedience," said Laura, furious with reaction and nearly crying herself. "I'll never bring you to see Lord Stoke again."

Master Wesendonck, who had made his way down the bank more carefully, now joined them with two small draggled peacock's feathers in his hand and looked on with interest.

"Dear, dear," said Lord Stoke, "your boy has had a nasty fall. Come back to the house, Mrs. Morland, and Ford shall look at him."

"Pull the skin off over his head if I had my way," said Dr. Ford unsympathetically. "Get on in front, you two. If you mother weren't here, Tony, I'd thrash you for frightening her like that."

Tony walked on in offended silence, followed by Master Wesendonck and the rest of the party. Halfway up the hill he began to limp heavily.

"Don't be a fool," snapped Dr. Ford.

He had not particularized in what direction folly was to be checked, but Tony apparently took the remark to heart, for he dropped the limp and walked easily onwards. When they got to the house Dr. Ford tended Tony with unloving hands and put a piece of strapping on his forehead, while Master Wesendonck looked on with envy and admiration.

"And mind you," said Dr. Ford, "I'm only doing this to please your mother and Lord Stoke. If you were my child I'd let you fester and gangrene, and serve you right. Did I or did I not tell you not to go near Stokey Hole?"

"Well, sir," said Tony, in a kind, explanatory voice, "we didn't go to Stokey Hole on purpose. We only saw the gate to the underground passage open, so Donk dared me to go in and I dared Donk. So when we got in it was dark and we had to use our torches to explore, and then we found the way out on to the bank. I say, that's a ripping bandage, sir," said Tony, looking at himself in a mirror with undisguised admiration. "I wish I could keep it on till next term. I could boast to the chaps at school about falling down a precipice."

"Cela n'empêche pas," said Dr. Ford.

"I know. Oh, Dr. Ford, could I see Sibyl's baby vaccinated now that I've got a bandage on? She would love to see me."

"Tony, Robert," called Mrs. Morland from the hall. "Time to go home."

Tony limped across the hall to where his host was standing.

"Hello, my boy," said Lord Stoke, "hurt your foot? Bad plan to go falling down banks, you know."

"I know, sir. Goodbye, and thanks most awfully for having us and for the feathers. Donk is awfully pleased with the feathers, aren't you, Donk?"

Master Wesendonck ducked his head at his host and shook hands in an embarrassed way. Tony laid his hand on his friend's shoulder for support and made his way heavily to the car.

"Hadn't you better look at Tony's foot?" said Laura anxiously to Dr. Ford as they followed the little boys.

"There's nothing wrong with it. He's only showing off."

Laura's face showed such a struggle between relief and resentment that Dr. Ford couldn't help laughing.

"All right; I'll come up tomorrow if you are really worrying," he said.

Laura then had to give her attention to subduing Tony, who had embarked on an interesting conversation with Albert under the butler's disapproving eye.

"You really mustn't make Albert laugh, Tony," she said when they had got home and were sitting at tea. "You see, he is supposed to behave very well when he is on duty."

"I know. Mother, Albert's an awfully decent chap. He's going to get some more peacock's feathers for me and Donk."

"By the way, what happened to the treat you were taking for the peacocks, Tony?"

"The treat, mother? Oh, the *treat*. Well, you see, it isn't a good plan to waste things, so Donk and I ate it in the car coming home. Can I have some more cake, please, mother? A really decent slice, please, because I'm so hungry."

CHAPTER 4

GREEN PEAS

In the night the weather changed. Laura woke to a cold wind pushing her window curtains out into the room, bringing with it sudden spurts of rain. It was only half-past seven, and she lay crossly in bed, telling herself that she ought to get up and shut the window before the dressing table was deluged. Another part of her urged her to stay in bed till Stoker brought her tea at eight o'clock, and then to tell Stoker to clear up the mess. The mental turmoil induced by this dual personality was so violent that she relapsed into an exhausted and uneasy sleep, from which she was roused by a knock on the door. Thinking that it was Stoker, she called out "Come in," without opening her eyes. The door opened and a soft paddy footstep, very unlike Stoker's assured and earth-shaking tread, approached her bed. A finger prodded her shoulder. Laura turned around and opened her eyes upon Master Wesendonck in his dressing gown, bearing a small piece of paper. He waited till she sat up and then pushed the piece of paper at her.

"What on earth is this?" asked Laura. "Draw the curtains, please, Robert, and shut the window. The rain's pouring in."

Master Wesendonck obeyed. While he was shutting the window and knocking a jar of face cream off the dressing table, Laura read the letter which ran as follows:

Dear Mother,
  I have been awake for hours because of my foot, Please need I get up.
This is urgent. Also could I have breakfast in bed.
      (Singed),   Your loving son,
                    A. MORLAND.

So used was Laura to thinking of her youngest son as Tony that it always came as a shock to her when his name appeared, usually more than half way down the class lists, as Morland, A. However, there was no mistaking the ill-formed writing, nor the general air of greyness which pervaded any paper that Tony wrote on.

"What's the matter with Tony's foot, Robert?" she asked. "Is it really hurting him?"

Master Wesendonck nodded.

"All right, I'll come along," said Laura. "Go and tell him."

Master Wesendonck left the room without shutting the door. The casement window, which he had imperfectly secured, blew open with a crash. A pane fell tinkling on to the flags below, while the curtains flew out like banners into the room and a pile of papers on a table were scattered all over the floor. Laura angrily put on her dressing-gown and slippers, shut the window properly, and went into Tony's room.

Morland, A. was sitting up in bed with a cheerful face and one leg stretched in front of him outside the bedclothes. His pajama leg was pulled up and his ankle was wrapped in a large woollen scarf.

"Oh, mother," said Tony, "I needn't get up, need I?"

"What's that on your leg?" said his mother.

"Oh, mother, that's a bandage, I thought I'd better have a bandage, so Donk tied the scarf around it. He's jolly good at bandaging, mother."

Without a word Laura removed the scarf. Tony's ankle was undoubtedly a little puffy, and when she touched it he evidently had to exert real, if ostentatious, self-control. Laura considered. Her first feeling was naturally annoyance with Tony. He had gone into Stokey Hole against orders, fallen down a bank through showing off, and

then most unjustly managed to have a real sprain. Her second feeling
was annoyance with Dr. Ford for minimizing her son's injuries.

"Well, I suppose you'd better stay in bed," she said grudgingly. "Dr.
Ford said he would come this morning."

"And can Donk have breakfast in bed with me, mother?"

"No. Stoker can bring you up some breakfast. You get dressed,
Robert; it's nearly breakfast time."

When she got down Laura told Stoker to put Tony's breakfast on
a tray, as he had hurt his ankle and was to stay in bed till Dr. Ford
came.

"I'd have sprained ankles if I was to lay in bed of a morning instead
of getting on with my work," said Stoker. "I'll take him up a nice
breakfast. Feed a cold and starve a fever, as the saying is. Shall I ring
up Dr. Ford?"

"Yes, do, Stoker," said Laura, secretly glad that Stoker had made
the suggestion.

Breakfast was consumed in silence while Master Wesendonck
victualled himself heavily for the morning's work and Laura read *The
Times*. Presently she heard Stoker go to the telephone.

"That you, Mrs. Mallow?" she heard her handmaiden say to the
doctor's housekeeper. "Well, then," continued Stoker's voice, "you tell
the doctor we've got our young gentleman in bed with something
wrong with his foot and there won't be no peace till the doctor comes,
so he'd better come here first, see?"

The reply appeared to be satisfactory, and Stoker came bursting
into the room carrying Tony's tray.

"Dr. Ford'll be around first thing," she said, walking through to the
kitchen. "Master Tony's ate up all his breakfast, so you haven't no call
to worry."

Dr. Ford shortly arrived in a skeptical mood, and was shown up by
Stoker to Tony's room, where his mother was trying to get him tidy
for the doctor's visit. As Master Wesendonck, with the kind object of
amusing the invalid, had already brought down from the playroom
quantities of rolling stock and several dozen yards of permanent way,
the floor was a good deal encumbered.

"Here, boy, take some of that rubbish out of my way," said Dr. Ford, pushing aside a milk van, six curved rails and a corridor coach as he spoke. Master Wesendonck exchanged a martyr's glance with Tony and reverently lifted the offending toys to a spot six inches away. Dr. Ford sat down on Tony's bed, examined his ankle and ordered cold-water compresses.

"It won't do you any harm to keep quiet for a bit," he said. "No dashing in and out of bed, mind. He'll probably be quite all right tomorrow, Mrs. Morland, if you can keep him off his feet."

"It *was* a sprain after all, you see," said Laura, in whose breast Dr. Ford's unsympathetic treatment of her son on the previous day was still rankling.

"Sprain! He ricked his ankle, that's all," said Dr. Ford. "Any messages for Low Rising? I'm going there, now."

"Just love to everyone. No one is ill, are they?"

"No," said Dr. Ford, picking up his bag. "I'm only going to vaccinate Miss Coates."

"Can I and Donk come?" said Tony eagerly. "My foot is quite well enough and I could hop."

"You can't. You should have thought of that before you went into Stokey Hole," said Dr. Ford grimly. "Good-bye, Mrs. Morland. Keep him quiet if you can, and if you can't, don't worry."

The next hour passed quietly enough. Master Wesendonck, under Tony's supervision, laid out an elaborate railway system all over the bedroom floor. The beds made excellent tunnels, and Tony had the intense pleasure of watching the Windsor Castle as it repeatedly plunged into the bowels of the earth on one side of his bed, emerged on the other, and then sped across the floor to Master Wesendonck's camp bed, and so under its trestles to a terminus near the door. It was arranged by mutual consent that each enthusiast should shriek for the whistle when the train was under his own bed, and this went on very happily till about eleven o'clock, when Stoker, unable to make herself heard through the noise, opened the door abruptly and came in with a large tray.

"Gives me the headache the way you two young gentlemen do go on," she said, setting down the tray on Tony's bed.

"Mind my foot, Stokes," said the invalid, suddenly relapsing into weakness and pallor.

I'd mind your foot fast enough if it was mine," said Stoker cryptically. "I've brought up some biscuits and milk for you both, and here's a basin of peas you can shell for me. Give you something to do, Master Tony, instead of laying there making that noise. Here's the colander. Put the peas in it when you've done them."

"Oh, Stokes, need I? My foot hurts."

"First time I ever heard of anyone shelling peas with their feet," said Stoker. "I'll put a fresh bandage on."

While Stoker, who appeared to confound the etymology of bandage and sandwich, wrung out the lint in cold water and put it on Tony's ankle, her patient slowly and miserably opened a few pea pods, put the peas into the colander with nerveless fingers, and fell back exhausted on the bed. Stoker, taking no notice of his weakness, went downstairs again.

About half an hour before lunch she remembered her peas and went up to Tony's room. Master Wesendonck, who was sitting on the floor with the colander on his head and a poker in his hand, looked at her with a threatening expression and pointed towards the bed. Several lengths of string had been tied from the head of the bed to its foot, and over these were hung Tony's sheets, forming a romantic and asphyxiating tent.

"What's that colander doing on your head, Master Robert?" said Stoker. "And where's my peas?"

Master Wesendonck looked towards the bed without opening his mouth. From a gap between the sheets Tony's face, very hot and damp, looked out.

"We needed a helmet, stoker," he said, "so I told Donk to put the peas in the basin in the bathroom and put some water on them to keep them cool, but the silly ass forgot to put the plug in, so they went swishing down the drain pipe."

"No peas for lunch then," said Stoker.

"Oh, but Stokes, there are all the other peas, the ones I didn't shell. I couldn't shell any more because of my bandage. I am King Arthur, Stokes, and Donk is my squire. King Arthur is a Southern Railway engine, a four-six-nought. Look at my tent, Stokes. I and Donk made it. Would you like to come in?"

"Give me them peas and I'll shell them myself," said Stoker, "and give me the colander, Master Robert, before I tell Mrs. Morland of you."

Laura then came in, vetoed Tony's suggestion that he and Donk should have their lunch in the tent together, and indeed showed so little sympathy as to order the tent to be dismantled.

"Rose and Dora are coming over as soon as they've finished lunch," she said, "and I don't want the room all in a mess."

"Oh, mother! Good on them! Mother, I'll let Rose and Dora see my bandage. What do you think they will say when they see it, mother?"

"I don't know. I shan't be in to tea, so you can all have it up here; only for goodness sake don't get into mischief."

"Mother," said Tony reproachfully, "how can I get into mischief? Don't you know that I've got a bandaged ankle?"

"Only too well," said his mother.

After lunch Master Wesendonck lay on the floor and drew pictures of dogs, while Tony, having demanded a pencil and an old exercise book, wrote with steady concentration. Laura went out in her car, and peace reigned in the sick room till Rose and Dora arrived.

"Hullo, Rose, hullo, Dora," said Tony. "I've got a bandage. I fell miles down the hill at Rising Castle and nearly broke my ankle. Dr. Ford had to come and see me and put a bandage on. You can see it if you like."

He stuck his leg proudly out of bed. The gentle Rose looked alarmed, but Dora's eyes gleamed.

"Did it bleed?" she asked hopefully.

"Not exactly, but it hurt like anything. I could hardly walk back to the castle. I have a great power of bearing things that other people can't bear. I bet you'd have yelled like anything if you'd had a bandage on your leg."

"Who is that?" asked Rose timidly, looking at Master Wesendonck.

"Oh, that. That's old Donk. He's a great friend of mine at school and I take care of him," said Tony patronisingly.

Rose and Dora said: "How do you do" politely, while Master Wesendonck ducked his head and shook hands in his usual hang-dog way.

"I've been writing a story," said Tony in an off-hand way. "Would you like to hear it before it's published?"

"Oh, Tony, is it going to be a real book?" asked Rose.

"Probably."

"Can I see it when it's a book?"

"Certainly. I shall have about a thousand copies in my Morland library and I'll give you one for Rosebush. You can have one for the Dorland library too if you like, Dora."

"My library is pretty full with my own books," said Dora carelessly.

"I know. But nobody reads your books. The Morland people read my books all the time. In fact a thousand copies aren't half enough. I shall have a cheap edition," said Tony, vaguely remembering conversations between his mother and Adrian Coates. "Now I'll read you my story. Oh, I'm King Arthur, and Donk is my faithful squire."

"Can I be a faithful squire too?" asked Rose eagerly.

Tony considered while Rose hung on his reply.

"You can be a squire if Donk doesn't mind," he said. "But Donk must be head squire."

"I am a queen," said Dora.

"That's simply invention," said Tony. "Now I'll read you my story."

The little girls and Master Wesendonck sat down on the floor and Tony was just about to begin, when the door opened and the whole party from Low Rising came in.

"Well, Tony," said Mrs. Knox, "how's the foot? Dr. Ford told us about it, so we came over to enquire."

Rose and Dora bore the greeting of the grownups with equanimity. Tony had an old dressingtable with drawers on each side and a kind of cave between them. Into this cave Master Wesendonck retreated and there curled himself up like an animal to watch the proceedings.

"I was just going to read a story aloud," said Tony. "Would you all like to hear it?"

"If it isn't too long," said Adrian.

"It is what you would call a suitable length. It is called 'Dick Montfort, or the Hero of the Sixth.'"

"The title seems familiar," said Adrian.

Tony looked at him suspiciously.

"I know," he said. "It begins——"

"One moment," said George Knox, who was seated on the foot of Tony's bed, "do I understand that this is a tale of public-school life?"

"Yes, sir. It is about a boy called Dick Montfort, who was the Hero of the Sixth."

"Enough," said George Knox. "Anne, my dear, I shall go to the drawing room and there await you. There is something about school stories peculiarly repellent to the adult intellect. I hold no brief for my own books, far from it, but they are at least not characterized by paucity of invention, improbability of incident, monotony of plot and entire want of taste. No, my boy, deeply as I admire your mother, I cannot bear, I positively refuse to bear, the rehearsal of a story which, considering your age and mental powers, cannot be other than derivative and altogether immature. Besides which I have already today endured sufficient mental torture in the conversation of that wholly delightful and competent Nurse Chiffinch. Anne," shouted George Knox to his wife in a sudden access of fury, "if that woman calls me poor grandpa again I will not be responsible for my actions. Am I to be called poor grandpa before my own granddaughter, as if I were the village idiot?"

"No, George," said his wife, "you aren't. But really there are rather a lot of us here, so I will come down with you while Tony reads his story to Adrian and Sibyl."

Tony waited patiently till the Knoxes had left the room, and then began again.

"Dick Montfort, or the Hero of the Sixth. Ha said Dick Montfort.

He drew a small wireless set from his pocket and listened in. Are you there said his brother's voice. I am said Dick. I am trapped by brigands said his brother can you drive my car for me at Brooklands in the great race. I can said Dick. He waited till night and pinched the science master's push bike and rode to Brooklands and won the race. Oh, Mr. Coates, did Dr. Ford vaccinate the baby?"

"Yes."

"I bet she yelled," said Tony. "I wish I'd been there."

"As a matter of fact she didn't make a sound," said Adrian, all up in arms on his daughter's behalf.

"Oh, Adrian darling," said Sibyl, "how can you say that? You weren't even in the room."

"Nor were you, darling."

"Well, darling, I was in the next room and you were only in the library. She was terribly brave, but just once I did hear her voice. It was just when Dr. Ford made the little scratch on her arm. Nurse says she has never had a baby that was so brave and splendid about it."

"Now I'll read you some more," said Tony in a loud voice. "Ha said Dick that night I must rescue my brother. He had three friends which were an Indian Prince and the boy who was the best boxer in the school and a very fat boy called Podge."

Here he paused dramatically and not in vain. Rose and Dora giggled at his wit, and he proceeded with a self-satisfied expression.

"They pinched the head master's car and drove to the lonely barn and rescued the brother. Next morning the head master said to Dick I must give you the cane for pinching my car, but just then the police had got the bandits and they came to the school to congratulate Dick. So he got off his caning and went into the Air Force. The end. What do you think of it, sir?"

"Well, it's a bit inconsecutive, but there is plenty of character and incident," said Adrian. "Speaking professionally, though, I don't see much commercial future for it."

"I know. Do you think I could get it published, sir?"

"I'd wait a bit," said Adrian.

"Donk thinks it's awfully good," said Tony. "I read him bits while I was writing it. Donk is going to draw a dog for illustrations."

"Where does the dog come in?" asked Adrian. "I didn't notice a dog in your story."

"I know. It was the head master's dog. I'll put in a bit about the dog when I publish the story."

"Can I see the dog drawing?" asked Dora.

Master Wesendonck thrust a piece of paper out of his cave.

"That's not a bit like a dog," said Dora contemptuously.

Rose, whose kind heart was always anxious for her friends, here came up to Sibyl and whispered to her, "Tony's friend is rather unhappy, I think, Mrs. Coates."

Sibyl looked towards the dressing table. From underneath it came the regular and irritating sound of someone sniffling.

"What is the matter?" she asked kindly.

"I think," said Rose to Sibyl, "it's about your baby being vaccinated, Mrs. Coates. He didn't like hearing about your baby being hurt."

"He's a baby himself," said Dora scornfully. "Fancy minding about a baby being vaccinated."

On hearing this Master Wesendonck crawled vengefully out from under the dressing table. Sibyl was afraid that he was going to bite Dora's legs, but he contented himself with gnashing his teeth at her in a very bloodthirsty way and making horrible faces. As Sibyl was getting no support from Adrian, who was reading Tony's manuscript with an absorbed face, she asked Master Wesendonck if he would like her to run him over to Low Rising in the car, so that he could satisfy himself that the baby was safe and happy. He made no reply, but coming to her side slipped his hand into hers and began to drag her from the room. Sibyl, seeing Rose looking wistful, invited her to come too.

"I'll not be more than a quarter of an hour, and I'll bring the car for you and Anne and Daddy," she said to Adrian.

"All right, darling," said Adrian. "I say, Tony, you ought to polish up your spelling. I admit that 'friends' is a difficult word, but it happens so often that you might learn it. And 'lonely' has an 'e' in it, and I suggest that 'Podge' represents the name of your fat boy better than 'Poge.'"

"I know. Mr. Coates, do you think I could be a publisher when I am grown up?"

"Possibly. What is the attraction?"

"I'd like to sit at a desk and press a lot of buzzers and bully people."

"What about book debts and overhead charges?" said Adrian.

"I am getting so tired of having a bandaged ankle," said Tony, ignoring Adrian's remark. "Will this day never finish?"

Adrian was so touched by Tony's blue eyes drowned in gentle melancholy that he offered to read aloud to him, and was justly punished for his kindness by having to read one of the school stories on which Tony had obviously modelled his own style, while Dora picked out tunes on a dilapidated toy zither which she had found in the toy cupboard, using Tony's nail scissors as a hammer. From this purgatory Adrian was rescued by the return of Sibyl with Rose and Master Wesendonck, and a second visit from the Knoxes to say goodbye to Tony.

"Come and see us as soon as your foot is well," said Mrs. Knox.

"Mrs. Coates' baby is quite happy," said Rose ecstatically.

Master Wesendock said nothing, but blew a few joyful blasts on his mouth organ, which encouraged Dora to make more noise on the zither.

"Goodbye, my boy," said George Knox. "Continue your literary lucubrations, though lucubrations is a singularly unsuitable description of the productions of one who works, I imagine, almost entirely by daylight, his bedtime being, I suspect, fixed at a comparatively early hour by those in authority, who, much as their natural affections would lead them to indulge him in keeping late hours, must nevertheless—are nevertheless—do nevertheless—What the dickens am I talking about, Anne? It is the result of that infernal noise, that brainless strepitation, produced by those devilish children there on the floor. Their noise bewilders me, it renders clear thinking an impossibility. My thoughts become involved, lost in a labyrinth without a clue, a labyrinth of which I, unhappily, am the miserable and hopeless center. Were I the fabled Minotaur, able to devour my victims —"

"Semi virumque bovem, semi bovemque virum," said Tony in his ringing Shakespearean voice.

"What the dickens are you talking about?" said George Knox, annoyed at this interruption to his period.

"Oh, sir, don't you know that? Don't you know Ovid, sir? That's part of the description of the Minotaur. The Minotaur lived in a labyrinth, sir. It means —"

But George Knox had fled, and was followed by his family, who all left their love for Laura. As soon as they had gone Stoker brought up tea and the invalid and his friends made a hearty meal.

"I'll tell you what," said Tony, "we'll have a band. Donk can play the mouth organ and Dora can do the zither and Rose can have a comb and paper and I'll sing."

Accordingly this unusual combination of instruments performed music, instrumental and vocal, with great spirit and vigor for quite half an hour. Tony, who had always firmly refused to indulge his mother by trying to sing songs for her, possessed a remarkable bellow which he was able to turn on at will, and the gentle Rose was transformed by her comb and paper to a howling Mænad. Laura had been in the room for a minute or two before any of the children noticed her presence.

"Hullo, mother," said Tony, "did you hear me singing? I sang jolly well. When I sing at school I somehow seem to sing above the other chaps. There's only one other boy at school that's better than me. He is a Burmese chap; his people live in Burma, and he has two throats."

"He can't, Tony."

"But, mother, he has. He told all the chaps that he has two throats. He says everyone who is born in Burma has two throats, and that's why he can sing so loud."

"Well, you do pretty well with one throat, Tony," said his mother. "Rose and Dora, you must go home now, your mother is expecting you, so say goodbye."

"Goodbye," said Tony, losing all interest in his guests.

Master Wesendonck scowled at Dora, but gave Rose a hearty and painful handshake, expressive of silent sympathy about Sibyl's baby.

"Mother," said Tony when they had gone, "can I get up for supper?"

"No."

"Well, can I make my bed into a tent again and have supper in it?"

"No. But you can go and have a bath while I make your bed again. Robert can help you to hop to the bathroom."

Tony sprang out of bed onto his uninjured foot and with his friend's assistance hopped off to the bathroom. Laura turned back Tony's bedclothes and rescued from among the crumpled sheets two pencils, half a biscuit, three cigarette cards and a piece of chewing gum, which she laid on the table by his bed. Then she turned the mattress and began to make up the bed again, but her mother's ear was gradually becoming conscious of some kind of abnormal noise in the bathroom. She could hear Tony's voice giving Master Wesendonck instructions and the occasional clink of metal on metal. At last her fearful curiosity became too great to bear, so she went across to the bathroom and opened the door. Tony was sitting in the steaming bath, peacefully employed in filling the largest sponge with water and putting it on his head, so that water ran down his face. Master Wesendonck was kneeling down in front of the fixed basin, mysteriously employed.

"What are you doing, Robert?" said Laura.

Master Wesendonck turned around and stretched out towards his hostess an extremely dirty hand with a number of round slime-covered objects on it which Laura identified to her surprise as peas. She then became aware that Master Wesendonck's other hand held a spanner, that screw plug at the bottom of the waste pipe below the basin had been removed, and that the floor was covered with very unpleasant grey, sloppy dirt.

"What are you doing?" she asked again.

"It's the peas, mother," said Tony.

"What peas?"

"Well, mother, Stokes wanted me to shell the peas for her, and I did shell a few, and then I got too tired, so I told Donk to put them down in the basin and put the water on them till I was untired enough to shell some more. You always ought to put peas in water when they are shelled mother, didn't you know that?"

"I did."

"Well then, mother, Donk was such an ass that he forgot to put the plug in, so when he turned the tap the peas simply swished down the drain pipe. But I have a kind of instinct about drain pipes, mother, and I knew this pipe was pretty well choked up."

"Yes, and who choked it up," said his exasperated mother, "putting all those bits of soap down it last week?"

"I know. But, mother, soap always melts. So I told Donk to get a spanner out of the car and take the screw off the U-joint. Mother, do you know what a U-joint is?"

"I knew long before you were born."

"And it was gorgeous," said Tony, with shining eyes. "When Donk got the screw off, all the squelchy stuff came plopping out and we got out all the peas. There's heaps more squelch up the pipe. Show mother, Donk."

Master Wesendonck thrust his fingers up the pipe and withdrew them encrusted with grey filth, which he gloatingly exhibited to his hostess. At that moment Stoker came into the bathroom.

"Look," said Laura.

"That's all right," said Stoker. "That pipe wanted cleaning, anyhow. The waste's not been running not like what it ought since Master Tony put all the soap down last week. I'll get a pail and clear up a bit."

"Can we have the peas for supper?" asked Tony, who was now wrapped in a large bath towel.

"No, Tony, they are perfectly disgusting."

"Oh, mother, but I took all the trouble to shell them, and now you want me to waste them."

Stoker said nothing, but she winked portentously at Tony and put the peas in her apron pocket.

"You had better have your bath now, Robert," said Laura, pushing her hair off her forehead with an exhausted gesture, "and Stoker can bring you both up your suppers in bed."

Half an hour later she went up to Tony's room. The little boys were eating their supper. Master Wesendonck paused occasionally between mouthfuls to woo the muse on his mouth organ, and Tony was reading a book.

"Have you had a nice supper?" said Laura, sitting down on Tony's bed.

The student lifted his eyes from his book.

"Supper?" he inquired abstractedly. "Oh, *supper*. Yes, thank you, mother."

"You'd better stay in bed till Dr. Ford has seen you tomorrow."

"Oh, mother, need I? Mother, this has been a long, sad day of melancholy and misery."

"Rubbish."

"But, mother, it has, truly. Oh, mother, can't I get up tomorrow?"

Laura's foolish heart melted as usual.

"Very well," she said resignedly, "but try to be careful."

"Donk," said Tony, suddenly becoming the stern man of action, "chuck over those peas."

Master Wesendonck paused in his music to throw at Tony's bed a dirty handkerchief knotted at one corner.

"What is that for?" asked Laura as Tony began to untie the handkerchief.

"Its' the peas we got out of the drain pipe, mother. Stokes cooked them for our supper, and there were ten each, so I betted Donk I could get up tomorrow and if you said yes I could have his peas. If you said no, I had to give him my peas."

As he spoke he drew from under his pillow an envelope with green stains on it. Into this he shook Master Wesendonck's forfeited peas, and before his horrified mother could stop him he had emptied the whole contents of the envelope into his mouth.

"Oh, I forgot to tell you, mother," he said with his mouth full, "Donk dropped your spanner out of the window into the water butt. He only did it by mistake, so I told him not to worry, because you wouldn't mind a bit."

CHAPTER 5

PARADISE POOL

Master Wesendonck's stay was drawing to an end. Laura, who thought Tony ought to have young companionship, had asked him whether he would like to invite his friend to stay for another week.

"Donk's a jolly decent chap, mother," said Tony, putting a drop of oil into the works of the Windsor Castle, "but I think one needs a little rest from people sometimes. Besides, Donk's baby sister will be needing him."

Laura was secretly delighted, for though Master Wesendonck had been an almost ideal guest—quiet, polite and docile—she had never quite known what would happen next. Some subtle chemical reaction continually took place between him and Tony, which automatically produced trouble. The last fortnight had been a series of minor anxieties and mishaps. No sooner was Tony's ankle well than he and Master Wesendonck had climbed on to the Vicarage roof just before evening service, a thing which neither of them would have attempted to do alone. Even so, all might have been well and their escapade not discovered, had not Master Wesendonck let his mouth organ slip down the roof into a gutter. His outcries had roused the household. The Vicar had come out in great fury, Mrs. Gould had begged them to stay where they were till the gardener could be fetched from his cottage and get a ladder, while Rose and Dora had hopped admiringly from one foot to the other and added their screams to the Vicar's objurgations and Mrs. Gould's entreaties. Luckily the gardener was a nephew by marriage of Mrs. Mallow and a great friend of Tony's, so he had waited till the Vicar had rushed off fuming to the church, and then rescued the mouth organ, while Tony and Master Wesendonck had returned as they came, by a route which involved a dirty trap door and a loft full of spiders' webs and dust. Laura had not been present at this scene, but the disgusting state of the little boys' shirts and knickerbockers, and Tony's grossly exaggerated account of the dangers they had run, made her feel thankful that she and Tony would soon be alone.

"What shall we do for Robert's last day?" she asked at breakfast. "Shall we have a bathing picnic and see if Sibyl and Adrian can come, and Rose and Dora?"

"Well, mother, did think of writing some more of my book today. I thought Donk would like to hear it before he goes."

"You can write just as well out of doors, Tony. Bring your writing book in the car. I'll go and ring up Mrs. Gould and Sibyl."

Adrian and Sibyl were delighted to come, and agreed to meet Laura and her party at Rushmere Pool, away on the other side of Rising Castle. Mrs. Gould accepted with enthusiasm for Rose and Dora, and then hesitated.

"I wonder if you could manage one more," she said. "The two elder girls are down here for their holiday. Ruth is going to play tennis with friends, but Sylvia has nothing to do today and she would so love a bathing party."

Stoker had put a poor opinion of what she called "those two Vicarage girls," blaming them loudly for not having found husbands at their ages, but Laura liked them both, especially Sylvia, the elder. She could not agree with Stoker that to be games mistress at a large girls' school at the age of twenty-three was necessarily the prelude to a life of depressing spinsterhood. So she assured Mrs. Gould that they would be delighted to have Sylvia, and went to consult Stoker about a picnic lunch.

"There will be three from the Vicarage," she said. "Miss Sylvia and Rose and Dora."

"I suppose you'll be having Dr. Ford then," said Stoker.

"I shouldn't think so, Stoker. He hasn't time for picnics."

"All right. But you mark my words," said Stoker impressively, "it isn't for nothing that Mrs. Mallow gets her old age pension next year."

"Well, I don't know what you are talking about, Stoker. We shan't want a big lunch; it's so hot. Hard boiled eggs, perhaps, and some tomatoes and bread and butter——"

"Don't you worry. I'll make a nice lunch, something the young gentlemen will fancy," said Stoker. "And did you wish Master Tony and Master Robert to bark at the postman before breakfast?"

"Bark at the postman?"

"Yes, that's what they done the last two mornings. Hide behind the gate they do, like as if they was dogs, and come out barking. The postman said it gave him a turn and he wasn't going to put up with it, so I thought you'd like to know."

Laura, reflecting that the things servants thought one would like to know were always those which one would most gratefully ignore, left Stoker to deal with the lunch and went in search of the little boys. She found them hanging over the edge of the water-butt, poking about with sticks.

"Mother," said Tony, "you know that spanner that got into the water-butt the day I had my bandaged ankle? It's here; we can feel it. Can I put on my bathing dress and grabble it up with my feet?"

"No. The water is full of snails and dead leaves and things, and you'll smell of it all day. I'll tell Sid Brown to get it out when he comes around to do the garden after his work. Listen. You and Robert mustn't bark at the postman, or we shall get into trouble."

"Bark, mother?" said Tony, with such candor that his mother was as usual nearly deceived. "Oh, you mean *barking*. Well, mother, we thought as you won't have a dog you would like us to pretend you had one. Of course, if the postman doesn't like dogs, it's all no good."

"Sylvia is coming today," said Laura. "She will be here with Rose and Dora quite soon, so go and get clean and get your bathing things."

Tony's face lit up rapturously as she began to speak, but by the time she had finished he was plunged in gloom.

"I thought you meant Mrs. Birkett's Sylvia," he said, mournfully, alluding to the golden cocker spaniel belonging to his head master's wife. "Darling, Sylvia, I wish it was her and not Rose and Dora's Sylvia. Mrs. Birky's Sylvia would be heavenly on a picnic, mother. She can swim beautifully."

"I expect this Sylvia can too," said his mother. "You know she teaches swimming at the school where she is. You ought to practice with her. She taught Rose and Dora, and they are very good."

"They can get along pretty well," said Tony grudgingly, "but their style is rotten, mother. Donk is pretty rotten, but I'll give him a few hints, won't I, Donk?"

Master Wesendonck tried to get Tony's head into chancery, and both little boys rolled on the grass.

Hearing a car, Laura went around to the front door. Dr. Ford's two-seater was there with Sylvia Gould in front and Rose and Dora jumping up and down in the dicky seat.

"I hear you are having a picnic," said Dr. Ford. "Where are you going?"

"Rushmere Pool. I would have asked you, but you are always busy."

"I'm doing the hospital at Southbridge this afternoon, but I needn't be there till three. If I happen to pass the Pool about one or half past, would you have a mouthful to spare?"

"Oh, sir," said Tony, who had wriggled free of Master Wesendonck's hold and come around to see what was happening. "Oh, sir, how is the baby's vaccination?"

"Splendid. Have you said how do you do to Sylvia?"

"Hello, Sylvia," said Tony, "hello, Rose, hello Dora. Is the baby's arm a sight, Dr. Ford? Stoker said it would be, and she says her little niece took so badly they had to have her arm off."

"Well, you needn't expect anything so interesting from Sibyl's baby. It's just a plain, straightforward case."

"That will be a great relief to Donk, sir. Hi, Donk, Sibyl's baby is quite all right. Come on and get the bathing things."

Dr. Ford drove off on his rounds and gradually Laura got the party under way. The lanky Rose was bodkin in front between Laura and Sylvia, while Tony, Master Wesendonck and Dora packed into the back with the lunch. Sylvia Gould was a tall handsome young woman, with fair hair, and skin tanned to an exquisite pale brown. Laura knew that she taught games at a school to help her parents, when she would much rather live at home in the country, and respected her for it.

"How is the school, Sylvia?" she asked.

"Pretty good, thanks. I may be getting something better in the autumn, abroad. I hope so. Mother and Dad don't find things too easy with Rose and Dora getting so big. They had a pretty hard time last winter when Rose had pneumonia, but Dr. Ford was a brick and wouldn't take a penny. Still, the nurses cost something and I'm keen to help as much as I can."

The August sun poured down, making the car very hot, and Laura was glad when they turned off into the shady road that led to Rushmere Pool. Rushmere Brook, which had meandered peacefully through miles of meadow land, entered a narrow valley at this point. The lower end of the valley had been dammed up by a former Lord Stoke, and the brook had spread into a long shallow pool, overhung by beech trees. Near its upper end was a small grassy slope, consecrated by many picnics of Morlands and Knoxes, and to this they carried the food. It was not long before Adrian and Sibyl arrived, bursting with news about the baby which had taken the vaccination as no other baby had ever done before, or so Nurse Chiffinch said, and was altogether a most unusual person.

"Now, who is going to bathe?" said Laura. "The four children are, and you, Sylvia. I'm not. What about you two?"

"I will," said Sibyl. "Adrian doesn't want to."

"Will the children be quite safe without a man?" asked the Victorian Laura.

"I can save anyone's life and do artificial respiration," said Sylvia. Laura shuddered.

"Oh, mother!" said Tony. "As if we need anyone with us. Anyone would think we couldn't swim at all by the way you talk, mother. It's pretty rotten bathing here, though. Not a springboard anywhere. I'm used to a diving board in the school baths, of course. Mother, you haven't seen me do the crawl. I simply tear across the baths."

"Come on then and let's see you," said Sylvia. "Too much talking, Tony. Get down to facts."

Speechless with indignation, Tony took his towel and bathing dress and went off with Master Wesendonck.

"I hate bossy people," he confided to his friend as they undressed. "I bet she can't swim across the pool. I did six lengths in the baths last term. I have a kind of natural gift for swimming, just like animals."

"Now, Mrs. Morland," said Sylvia, "you must sit down and rest. I'll take Rose and Dora with me to undress. Don't worry about Tony and his friend. I often have to look after thirty children at once. Do you swim, Mrs. Coates?"

"Only in shallow water," said Sibyl. "I find one sinks so quickly in deep water."

Laura and Adrian sat down under a beech at the water's edge and waited for the bathers to reappear.

"How is everything?" he asked.

"Oh, just about ordinary, thank you. But you don't want to hear about my affairs, Adrian. You want to tell me about the baby."

"No, really, Laura. I want to hear about you. We haven't met for ages."

"If you mean, Am I writing a new book for you, I am. And if you mean, Can you see it, you can't. And all the boys are quite well, so that's that."

"But what about you, Laura? Are you still the solitary-hearted?"

"Lord bless my soul," said Laura, half amused, half angry, "what does that matter to you? It's just your passion for sentiment that makes you ask such silly questions."

"Sorry, Laura," said Adrian.

She gazed out across the pool. The dark green water mirrored the beech trees on the banks. High arching boughs shut out the sky. In that green valley there was no breath stirring.

"I suppose everyone is solitary-hearted," said Laura, thinking aloud and as usual finding considerable difficulty in formulating her thoughts. "If you are born lonely, you die lonely. I expect I'm rather lucky really, because though I sometimes nearly break my heart with loneliness, it is better than not being alone. But you are too young to understand that, Adrian," she added, with her charming tired smile.

Adrian had nothing to say. "I'm not," would be discourteous and untrue. For though being married doubtless gave one status, and definitely put one in the ranks of grown-up people, it had somehow made him feel younger where Laura was concerned. He used to feel like her contemporary. Now he felt like a very much younger brother.

"You see," Laura went on, frowning and hesitating over her words, "loneliness gets to be a bad habit, like taking drugs. I'm not very good at making friends—I'm a bit stupid and stiff—so I shut myself up with my own dull self and am not unhappy. Tony is my only key to things. Of course, I am very fond of you and George and a few other people, but your lives are going on: mine isn't. It went on very hard while the boys were all little. Then it got slower and slower. Now that three of them are independent, it is only about a quarter of what it was. When Tony is on his own it will stop. I don't mean that I'll put my head in the gas oven, but I'll be a dull hermit, less and less wanting to make any effort. I'll go on writing for you if you still want my books, because I feel a sense of responsibility towards you, but I shall hardly be there."

"Meanwhile there *is* Tony," Adrian hazarded.

"I know. If there weren't, there wouldn't be much reason for me."

"Laura darling, there would. Your friends—"

Laura shook her head.

"No, Adrian. I'm not very intelligent, but I can face facts. No one is really missed—except children. If Tony died—"

But this thought was too much for her, and she had to mop her eyes and blow her nose and push some hairpins farther into her head. Luckily Adrian was able to distract her attention by pointing out the bathers, who was coming from their dressing places to the water. They were a pretty sight among the green, Sylvia like a silver and bronze statue in her white bathing suit, with her two younger sisters in red and orange, Sibyl slim in green, Tony and Master Wesendonck with the brightly striped tops that school fashion demanded that year. Sylvia shepherded her flock to where Laura was sitting.

"I'm going to give the boys a good lesson," she said. "Rose and Dora don't swim badly, but Tony's style was shocking last time I saw him. I don't know about his friend. What is your name? Robert? Can you swim, Robert?"

Master Wesendonck shook his head and retreated.

"He can swim," said Tony, "because I taught him last year, but he doesn't like it."

"Rot," said Sylvia. "Come along, Robert, if that is your name, and I'll hold you up while you practice. I'll have you swimming in no time. Why are you wearing a cap? Boys don't wear caps."

Master Wesendonck cast a despairing glance around him. The other grown-ups were talking. Tony was taking far too dispassionate an interest.

Rose looked sorry for him, but Dora was obviously exultant. Master Wesendonck's behavior to her on the day when Tony had the bandaged ankle was still rankling, and she was delighted at his prospective downfall and disgrace at her sister's hands. She stood blowing up an indiarubber pig and gloating over his discomfiture.

"Come alone, Robert," said Sylvia, putting out an arm to grab him.

"Baby is going to swim," said Dora, with the devilishness of which only little girls are capable. She then danced around Master Wesendonck with a fiendish grin, added, "Nyang, nyang."

There is something about these meaningless words, especially when accompanied by a fiendish grin, which no person of spirit can bear. Master Wesendonck twisted out of Sylvia's grasp, seized Dora's indiarubber pig and dashed down the grassy slope into the water. Dora with a shriek of rage started in pursuit, but Rose, taller and fleeter of foot, caught her up and tried to stop her.

"Let me go," shrieked Dora. "Robert has taken my pig."

"Serve you right for being rude," said Sylvia, coming up and disentangling her little sisters. "You can't get the pig now, so you'd better come and practice your crawl."

By this time indeed Master Wesendonck was more than halfway across the lake. As they watched him he reached the farther bank and climbed out where a high rock jutted into the water, its top bathed in the sunshine that came through a gap in the trees. Shortly afterwards he appeared at the summit and sat down with his legs dangling over the edge. Here the exasperated Dora was able to see him slowly inflate her pig and place it beside him. He then took off the bathing cap which had so outraged Sylvia's code and drew from it his beloved mouth organ. Strains of music floated from his eyrie across the water.

"Did you really teach Robert to swim?" asked Sylvia, eyeing Tony doubtfully as he splashed violently in the water without making progress in any particular direction.

"He did have some lessons with the swimming instructor," said Tony, "but I really gave him confidence. It's a kind of gift I have to make people feel confidence. Donk got the swimming prize last term after I'd given him confidence."

"And have you confidence?" asked Sylvia.

"Of course. When you can swim you get confidence at once. Would you like to see me dive? It's pretty rotten, of course, having no diving boards here, but I can dive without a diving board. Look, Sylvia. Look, Rose and Dora. Watch for me to come up again."

With a loud shriek he put his hands above his head and prepared to dive. Sylvia, Rose and Dora watched with interest. Tony's head and shoulders disappeared into the lake, most of his back remained high and dry, while his legs churned the surface of the lake violently. Presently he was emerged.

"Did you see me dive?" he asked.

"It was lovely, Tony," shrieked the little girls.

"You can't dive at all," said Sylvia. "I must say I don't think much of the instructor at your school. I am going around the lake to see if there is a decent plane one can dive from, and if there is I'll give you a lesson."

"I told her it was rotten to have to dive without a diving board," said Tony to his sympathetic audience. "Come on and let's find a boat.

There's an old tree trunk under Donk's rock, and we can have a ship with it. Come on. I'll race you across."

Rose and Dora were off at once. When they reached the other side Tony was nowhere to be seen, but in a few minutes he came strolling along the path which bordered the lake. It had been hardly worth while to swim such a little way, he explained, and as it was a work of public value to explore thoroughly the surroundings of the pool, and no one seemed to be doing it, the duty fell upon him.

"There's a splendid bit up at the top," he said, "all black mud and squelch. We'll go there when we've finished making our boat. Hello, Donk."

Master Wesendonck answered with a chord.

The boat on which Tony had set his heart was an old water-logged trunk lying at the water's edge. After a quarter of an hour of pulling and pushing, ably directed by Morland A., they managed to get it into deep water, where it gently sank to the bottom.

"It's a German submarine," said Tony with bloodthirsty joy. "We've sunk it, and they are all dead. Donk!" he shouted, "do you see the German submarine? Everyone is drowned."

"Oh, no, Tony," said Rose, almost in tears, "let them escape."

"They can't. The doors are all jammed."

"No, they aren't," said Dora, taking her sister's part. "Twenty men got out before they jammed, and they are all swimming to the bank."

Master Wesendonck, who had been listening attentively to this dialogue, now flung Dora's pig from the top of his rock into the water. The meaning of his action was understood by Tony, who immediately realized that the pig was a depth charge.

"Good on you, Donk," yelled Tony. "It exploded underneath them and blew them all up. All their arms and legs and heads are blown off."

Rose began to cry. Dora, unable to reach Master Wesendonck, flung herself on Tony, but at that moment Laura's peahen call of "Lunch" came echoing across the water. Master Wesendonck came scrambling down from his rock with surprising rapidity, Dora rescued the pig, and the four children sped around the head of the lake, only pausing to get unnecessarily dirty in the squelchy mud.

Adrian and Laura, assisted by Sibyl, whose notion of bathing was to dabble at the water's edge, looking very pretty, and conversing with her husband and Mrs. Morland, had laid out lunch on the grass. It was all very delightful and uncomfortable. Caterpillars let themselves down from trees, flies crawled on the sugar, a wasp hovered angrily around them, nature was at its loveliest.

"Where is Sylvia?" asked Rose.

"Not drowned?" said the anxious Laura, whose general impression of water, fresh or salt, deep or shallow, was that it was always lying in wait to catch people and pull them under. Luckily for her fears voices were heard through the trees and Sylvia's white-clad form was seen approaching with Dr. Ford. Dr. Ford explained rather lengthily that he had seen Sylvia while he was parking his car and had come along with her. No one took much notice of his explanation, which seemed dull and unnecessary.

"Can you dive, Dr. Ford?" asked Tony.

"No. I've always been too frightened."

"Oh, sir. I can dive off the second highest diving board at school. You should see me, sir. It's a marvelous feeling to go flying through the air and splash into the water. You ought to try. I'll give you some hints."

"Shut up," said Dr. Ford.

"But what are you frightened of, Dr. Ford?" asked Sylvia.

"Infection of the middle ear for one thing."

"The middle ear?" said Tony nervously.

"Yes. It's a nasty thing."

"I know. But where exactly is it?" asked Tony, who had disturbing visions of an unsuspected ear somewhere at the back of Dr. Ford's neck, under his collar.

"Inside your head, and don't ask so many questions. I'm frightened of heights too, Sylvia."

Tony brooded over the horrid suggestion of another ear inside one's head. The grownups, all talking together, each related his or her reaction to heights. Adrian confessed to disliking the look of a lift shaft from the top, and Laura told him he needn't look down it. Sibyl said she always thought it would be very horrid to fall off something very high, because one would fall so far.

"I have terrifying dreams," said Laura, gaining the attention of her audience by using her deepest voice. "I dream I am on a very high tower and it begins to shake, and then I wake up."

"If you didn't wake up you'd be dead, mother," said Tony. "Stokes said so. She had a cousin that that happened to. I had a marvelous dream, mother, that I was on the Flying Cornishman, and when we went through Reading station the whistle blew so loud and we made such a rush of air that the whole station fell down and then the guard said: 'All change here for Quadratic Equation Junction.' It was marvelous, mother. Don't you think it's jolly good, Mr. Coates — Quadratic Equation Junction? I expect I had that dream because I was thinking about algebra. I'm pretty good at algebra, only there are about ten boys that have the gift of being better than me. I expect —"

"Stop talking, Tony," said his mother, "and get on with your lunch."

"Nyang, nyang," said Dora.

"Be quiet, Dora," said Sylvia.

"Wasp, wasp!" shrieked Rose.

A large wasp was crawling about on Rose's plate, enjoying the remains of a jam sandwich. As she shrieked it rose with an angry sound, flew around her head and settled again.

"It will sting me," wailed Rose.

"Here, Donk, this is where you come in," said Tony in an offhand way.

Master Wesendonck crawled over to Rose's place, seized the jam knife in a firm grip, and before anyone could stop him had cut the wasp in two at the waist. The front half walked about on the cloth, the back half twitched. Rose flung herself screaming into Laura's arms.

"Gosh, that was a good one," said Tony with unselfish pride in his friend's achievement. "Just look at the two bits, Dr. Ford. Donk is jolly good at cutting wasps in two. He cut six in two at breakfast last term and matron went off pop and reported him. I'd like to cut hundreds of wasps in two and have a huge funeral. Let's have a funeral, Donk."

"Certainly not," said Laura, comforting poor Rose. "You and Robert are nothing but a nuisance. Go and play somewhere."

"I suppose people like to have wasps stinging them," said Tony bitterly as he and Master Wesendonck strolled away around the lake. "Come on, Donk, let's explore."

Accordingly they walked around the head of the pool again, past the squelchy mud, but when they came to Master Wesendonck's rock he insisted on taking up his old position overlooking the water, and composing on his mouth organ. Tony walked on alone, his bare feet gratefully feeling every varied surface, the pleasant heat of rocky outcrops, the coolness of mud where the path dipped to the water, the homely feeling of bare earth. He was detained for some time by a small natural harbor at the water's edge, where one could sail bits of wood for battleships and watch rich black mud surge up between one's toes. Then he pursued his journey, whistling aloud to himself, till he reached the end of the pool. Here a single arch spanned the opening through which the little Rushmere Brook escaped, ultimately to join the Rising. Below the arch the ground fell away a little, with soft grass coming down to the edge of the stream. Tony walked onto the arch and stood there surveying the scene. At the far end he could see the grownups clearing up the remains of lunch. He yelled to Master Wesendonck on his rock and received a blast of music in reply. Then he retraced his steps and went down to the lower level. The grassy edge and the bubbling stream invited him to paddle. As he stood in the brook, enjoying the feeling of water dividing and rippling about his feet, he looked upwards through the arch and saw the green lake lying on the level of his eyes. It was a sudden miracle to see that sheet of water suspended above him. Everything he saw suddenly seemed as small, as clear, as magic as what he had sometimes seen through the wrong end of his mother's opera glasses. The colored figures far away, the high overshadowing beeches, the sun baked rock where his friend sat, were all as clear as a vision, as unreal as a dream. Chords of music drifting across the water added a charm to the lovely romance. Tony thought of theaters that he had been taken to, of books that gave one a glimpse of unexplored worlds, of poems that

one learnt by heart and said aloud at night to make oneself luxuriously
sad. The key to all this world lay in that semicircle of stone.

"Paradise Pool," he said softly to himself.

A cloud drifted across the sun, the magic faded for a moment and
he was free to go. So he jumped very hard on a projecting piece of
earth for the pleasure of seeing it fall into the water and make it
muddy, climbed back on to the arch, yelled hideously at Master
Wesendonck, and continued his way around the pool to the picnic
ground.

Here he was caught by Sylvia Gould, who had found a little rock
with some deep water below it and wanted the children to practice
diving. Rose and Dora were already at work, flying elegantly through
the air, cleaving the water with hardly a splash, and rising exactly
where they should. Sylvia took Tony to the edge of the rock and gave
him clear instructions as to how to take his dive.

"But, Sylvia," he expostulated, "I can't dive properly without a
diving board. I can dive splendidly at school because there is a diving
board."

"Then you can dive here," said Sylvia. "Off you go."

Tony fell incompetently off the rock, with his arms flapping
untidily and his legs doubled up under him.

"Did you see me dive?" he called out, as he came to the surface.

"Yes, and it was rotten," said Sylvia. "Come back and try again.
What were you doing with your legs?"

"Well, you see, I was afraid of kicking you. You were quite close
behind me, so I had an instinct to bend my legs in case I hit you when
I dived. As a matter of fact I could have done a very good dive, but—"

"That's enough," said Sylvia, who was used to standing no nonsense from a large swimming class twice a week. For the next quarter
of an hour Tony was bullied and browbeaten to an extent which he
could hardly believe. Every time he tried to talk Sylvia cut him off
short. She laughed at his explanations, refused to listen to his excuses,
held his arms and legs in the right positions, criticized every movement that he made, and worst of all made unfavorable comparisons
between him and the girls. To be beaten by Rose, who was taller and

older than himself, was bad enough, but to be outclassed by Dora, who was his junior and exactly his height, was degrading.

"Nyang, nyang," said Dora, who had not yet forgotten the affair of the depth charge, as Tony tumbled anyhow into the water for the eighth time, "who can't dive?"

Tony, ignoring her remarks, waded ashore and walked away. Dr. Ford, who had been watching, came up to Sylvia and congratulated her warmly.

"You are a woman in a thousand," he said admiringly. "When I think that you have done in a few minutes what a mother, three elder brothers, all Mrs. Morland's old friends and any number of schoolmasters and schoolfellows have failed to do in many years, I can only offer you my homage."

"What's that?"

"Talked Tony down."

"Tony? Oh, he's no trouble. If none of the children I have to teach were worse than he is, it would be an easy job."

Seldom had Dr. Ford said goodbye with more reluctance than to this admirable girl, who looked like a goddess and was a match for Tony Morland, but the hospital claimed his services. Before he went, however, he had arranged to come up to the Vicarage for bridge that evening.

Meanwhile Tony, swelling with rage and mortification, made his way for the third time around to the rock where Master Wesendonck, siren-like, was still enchanting the air.

"Hi, Donk!" he shouted, "I want you."

Master Wesendonck climbed down.

"Come on, Donk," said Tony, "I'm about fed up with people. Interfering beasts, trying to teach people to dive. Anyone knows that people can't dive without a proper spring board. It all comes of having girls on picnics. Come on, Donk, I've something to show you."

He led the way to the end of the pool. His friend followed him, and both little boys stepped down into the brook.

"Look," said Tony, pointing upwards to the arch.

It was evident, to Tony's infinite satisfaction, that the vision of the floating lake filled his friend with the same blissful nostalgia that he himself had felt. Master Wesendonck was gazing enchanted upon the magic pool suspended in midair, deeply conscious of its romance, awed by its unreal beauty.

"Paradise Pool," said Tony in a whisper.

Master Wesendonck nodded violently. Both little boys stood entranced, till Laura's voice was heard over the water, calling them by name. For a moment Tony thought of not hearing it, but the risks of grown-up people coming and finding his paradise were too great, so with a sigh he stepped onto the grass and turned towards the homeward path. Master Wesendonck followed him, with a vision, deep in his romantic silent being, of perhaps showing the pool to Mrs. Coates's baby when she was old enough to understand.

It was perhaps inevitable that the afternoon should end with anti-climax. Adrian and Sibyl took Sylvia back to tea and tennis at Low Rising. Laura asked the little girls to stay to tea, but bitterly was she to regret having done so. All four children were a little tired and over-excited, and the air was heavy with impending quarrels. It would be an exaggeration to say that Master Wesendonck was not on speaking terms with Dora, when he never spoke at all, but his whole attitude was scornful and offensive in the extreme. Tony and his friend joined together against Dora. Rose joined Dora against the little boys as a matter of principle, but she was also bound by loyalty to Master Wesendonck, owing to their feeling about Sibyl's baby, while Dora and Tony could not forget their normal state of truculent alliance against the gentle Rose. It was after tea that matters came to a head, when Tony proposed that they should blow up Dora's pig and use it for a football.

"You and Rose can look on," said Tony. "Girls can't play football."

"Well, boys can't dive," said Dora, "and you can't have my pig."

"Well, I jolly well can," said Tony. "And what's more, I *can* dive. Anyone will tell you that I can dive at school. In Morland I have a bath a hundred yards long and it's twenty feet deep at the deep end, and it has a diving board forty feet high and a water chute, and you can't come to it because girls aren't allowed."

Here he stopped to take breath and blow up the pig.

"Aren't I allowed?" asked Rose.

"Sometimes."

"And can Robert come?"

"Yes, Donk can come, and everyone except Dora."

"I don't want to come," said Dora. "Give me my pig."

"You couldn't come even if you wanted," said Tony, retreating from Dora and blowing the pig up hard between sentences. "You shan't come into Morland at all, ever. There will be submarines all around Morland, and sentries and live wires and airplanes."

At this juncture Master Wesendonck, inspired by hatred, became articulate for the first and last time in human knowledge.

"Dora Gould
Is jolly well fooled,"

he chanted in a hoarse exultant voice, accompanied by a shuffling movement from one foot to the other which was provocative in the highest degree. Rose gaped at him, open-mouthed with awe and admiration, while even the unimpressionable Dora was silenced. But rapidly recovering herself, she hurled defiance at the enemy.

"Anyway," said she carelessly, "Morland is all invention. Nyang, nyang."

At the same moment that Dora said these awful words Tony finished blowing up the pig and gave it a tremendous kick. It burst with a loud report. Master Wesendonck broke into wild mocking laughter. Dora, blind with fury, seized Master Wesendonck's mouth-organ and threw it over the hedge into the currant bushes. She then closed with Tony, while Rose burst into tears, and Master Wesendonck plunged through a flower bed and broke through a hedge in search of his beloved instrument. Laura came out and saw with horror her youngest son and the Vicar's youngest daughter in mortal combat. The disputants rushed to her with a storm of recriminations.

"Mrs. Morland, Tony burst my pig," cried Dora.

"Mother, she said Morland was an invention," cried Tony, his blue eyes flashing.

Laura, though hating them both equally for disturbing her peace, secretly felt that Dora's treachery about Morland was far worse than the unpremeditated destruction of a pig, but the code of a hostess forbade her to say so. She sent Tony straight to bed, comforted the overstrung Rose, and drove the little girls back to the Vicarage, where she delivered them to Mrs. Gould with many apologies for Tony's bad manners.

"I expect it's just as much their fault," said Mrs. Gould calmly. "Dora is a frightful nuisance sometimes. Don't make that noise, Rose."

"But Dora said Morland was an invention," sobbed Rose.

"Then you can both go to bed," said Mrs. Gould, who never tried to argue.

Tony went upstairs with an expressionless face, undressed, folded his clothes neatly, washed his face and hands, and got into bed. He was full of resentment against the world. People made one dive when one could really dive quite well if one had a proper diving board. If one killed a wasp people seemed to be annoyed instead of being grateful. People didn't even want one to bark like a dog, he thought, remembering earlier grievances. Girls were simply a nuisance and he was jolly glad he had burst Dora's pig. People who said "nyang, nyang" like that deserved to have their pigs burst. Even one's mother turned against one and sent one to bed. Self-pity overwhelmed Tony. His eyes pricked him and his throat swelled. He turned his face into the pillow and cried bitterly.

Presently he heard a faint sound of music proceeding from the kitchen garden. Old Donk had evidently found his mouth organ again and was expressing sympathy in his own way. Tony got up and looked out of the window, but the player was invisible. He opened a drawer, rummaged at the back of it, and found a stuffed donkey with a red flannel saddle, and a fox cub's brush much the worse for wear. With these he lay down in bed again and found that he was not crying so much. Fascinating and terrifying theories about the middle ear passed through his mind. Then a memory of the green pool with the sun shining through the trees came to comfort him. Again he walked by the side of the lake. Again he stood ankle-deep in Rushmere Brook and looked upwards through the arch. The vision was clear to him now, and his last waking thought was of Paradise Pool.

When Laura came in on tiptoe, heavy at heart for her little boy's punishment, she found him asleep, sprawling across his bed, the donkey and the fox cub's brush hugged in his arms. His eyes were still wet, but he looked deeply contented. Laura's own eyes filled with tears. She pulled a blanket over him and went softly from the room.

CHAPTER 6

A QUIET DAY AT HIGH RISING

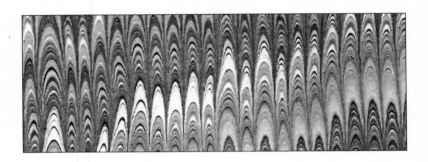

Breakfast had been on the table for ten minutes when Laura Morland looked up from her newspaper and saw that Tony's place was empty. Going to the foot of the stairs, she called her son's name loudly. There was no answer, but she heard the rushing sound of the bathroom taps, apparently turned full on, so she went upstairs to investigate.

"What are you doing, Tony?" she shouted through the locked door.

A muffled reply reached her which sounded like the word "charity," and after a moment's delay Tony, draped classically in a bath towel, opened the door and let her in. The bath was full almost to overflowing and both taps were still running furiously.

"I'm sorry I didn't hear you," said Tony, "but I was doing science. Look, mother."

With one bound he was back in the bath and at least a pailful of water came sloshing over onto the floor. His mother made for the taps and turned them off angrily.

"Get dressed at once and come down to breakfast," she said, "and wipe up that disgusting mess. And why are you having your bath now, anyway? Didn't you have one last night?"

"Of course I did, mother. But this is science. I thought you liked me to do science, in case I took up engineering."

"Come out at once."

"But, mother," said Tony, leaping joyfully up and down in the water, sending fresh deluges over the edge with every movement, "this is specific gravity. Don't you know specific gravity, mother? Archimedes discovered it. You fill the bath right up, and then you sit in it, and what comes over the edge is specific gravity."

In proof of his theory he leapt again like a salmon.

"Pull the waste pipe up and get out at once," said Laura. "And just mop up the water with your bath towel till Stoker can come."

She went downstairs and was presently rejoined by her son, who looked and felt uncommonly damp.

"Why are you so wet, Tony?" she asked.

"Well, mother, you said I was to mop up the water with my bath towel, so I had nothing to dry myself on except my shirt. Oh, mother, can I make a fountain in my porridge?"

He hastily made a hole in the middle of his porridge, and seizing the milk jug, poured a stream of milk into the hole from a height. The milk spurted up in an indubitable fountain, which showered its spray over the tablecloth.

"Put that jug down," said his mother, "and don't make any more messes. And don't make me say 'don't' again. It's too wet to do anything this morning. You can have Rose and Dora over to play if you like, only you must do some of your essay first."

"Oh, mother, need I? The other chaps don't do their essay till the end of the hols."

"Yes, you must. And this afternoon we are going to tea at the Vicarage. Don't dawdle now any more than you can help."

The essay was a holiday task inflicted by Mr. Prothero for no particular reason that his pupils could ascertain. The subject was "What I would do if I had a hundred pounds," and Mr. Prothero fondly hoped to get some insight into the character of his young pupils by its means. Needless to say the wittier spirits had agreed to invent various preposterous ways of using the imaginary windfall, choosing those most calculated to annoy Mr. Prothero, who was known to have Socialist leanings. The Form Prig had announced his intention of putting his into the Post Office Savings Bank till it had doubled itself, and then giving it to a hospital.

"You'd be dead long before that," said Tony contemptuously.

"Well, I wouldn't. Money doubles itself frightfully quickly. You'd be surprised how fast it gets doubled if you know anything about compound interest."

"I know," said Tony, "but it all depends on how much interest. I bet you don't know how much interest you get in the Savings Bank."

"I bet you don't either."

"Well, I bet your bet's wrong."

But at this moment Mr. Prothero, the sneaking beast, had given them both a hundred lines of Xenophon to write out for talking in class. So Tony, who wrote Greek neatly and prettily, had written out all the lines for them both, and the Form Prig had given Tony a key to unlock railways carriages with, and everyone was satisfied, including Mr. Prothero, who never noticed that Tony had written the same five lines twenty times over.

When he had finished breakfast Tony went into the drawing room and balanced himself on the arm of a chair till his mother asked him what the matter was.

"Well, mother, I thought you wanted me to write my essay."

"So I do. You can have the table by the window. The inkstand needs refilling. You know where the jar of ink lives. And be careful, and don't talk to me, because I'm trying to write."

Tony fetched the large stone jar of ink and filled the inkstand carefully. As he was replacing the cork Stoker came into the room.

"What did you do with that kipper I gave you for your breakfast, Master Tony?" she asked.

"I ate it, of course."

"Well, where's the bones? Left a lovely kipper hotting up over the spirit lamp for Master Tony," she said, gathering Laura into her audience, "and a cat or something must have got in, because there's none of it left."

"I ate the bones," said Tony, carrying the jar of ink back to its place under a bookcase.

"Tony!" said his mother.

"I always eat the bones, mother. I am like a dog. I have such good teeth that I can eat anything. I always eat the kippers' bones at school and matron goes off pop. I eat mine and the other chaps' too, sometimes. There's a chap at school that has a brother who eats chicken's bones, simply crunches them all up. I am starting practicing on kippers' bones to get into training for chickens."

"And what about the head?" asked Stoker.

Tony shuffled with his feet and kicked the jar of ink, which fell on its side. The cork came out and a sluggish stream of ink meandered along the floor.

"Good thing it's the boards and not the carpet," said Stoker genially. "We had enough mess with that iodine of yours, Master Tony. I'll wipe it up."

"Thank you, Stoker," said Laura. "Put the cork in properly, Tony, and get on with that essay."

For a quarter of an hour there was comparative silence. Laura's pencil rapidly and illegibly pursued the adventures of Madame Koska, the dressmaking heroine of her successful romances, through "The Affair of the Serpent Skin Bag." Tony twisted, writhed and moaned in the agonies of composition, but did not succeed in attracting his mother's attention. So Stoker's reappearance was as welcome to him as it was unwelcome to his mother.

"It's happened just like what I told you it would," said Stoker.

"What has?"

"Mr. Reid never sent them cooking apples last night, and how am I to get my pudding on in time? There was something told me he wouldn't."

"Well, I wish that something had told you to tell me before," said Laura. "Why don't you ring him up?"

"Have," said Stoker with pleasurable gloom, "and both the boys is out on the rounds."

"Well, Tony had better go," said Laura. "It's stopped raining now."

"Oh, mother, need I? Mother, I thought you wanted me to do my essay."

"Well, considering what a fuss you have been making over it," said his mother, "you ought to be glad of the excuse. Take a basket and go to Mr. Reid and fetch the apples, and you can ask Rose and Dora to come back with you. And don't dawdle."

When Tony had gone, his mother, moved by a sudden curiosity, went over to the writing table to inspect his essay. The state of the paper showed only too plainly that Tony had not put the cork back into the jar of ink without exercising the chemical attraction which exists between little boys and that useful fluid. The essay was evidently planned in the form of a narrative in the first person.

"One day," it began, "I was walking along the street when a man stopped me. What will you do he said if I gave you 100 £s? I received this remark cum grano salto and asked where it was. At home he said, but tell me first what you would do with the Mony if you had it. I said I would first give five lbs to my cher maman and buy a lot of bones to give to every dog I met. Well said the man, tell me some more. Not till I see the mony I said so he gided me—"

Here the fragment broke off.

"Jided? Oh, I see, guided. I suppose that's what I pay about a hundred and fifty pounds a year for," said Laura bitterly, and returned to her own literary work, about which she had no illusions whatever. But it helped to support her family, which was more, she reflected, than Tony's was likely to do.

Tony arrived at Mr. Reid's shop without more delay than was necessary to talk to a few dog friends of his.

"Got your basket, sir?" asked Mr. Reid.

"No. One simply couldn't carry a basket, Mr. Reid. What would people think? Can you put them in a bag?"

Mr. Reid accordingly put them into a large paper bag, cautioning Tony not to hold it by the top, as it might burst.

"Take it in your arms, sir," he said, "like a baby."

At this degrading suggestion Tony's face became quite expressionless. He took the bag by one corner and pursued his way towards the Vicarage. Outside the churchyard gate the bag burst and all the apples fell out.

"They would," said Tony aloud.

He picked them up and put them one by one down the neck of his jersey, which he was wearing belted inside his knickerbockers. Then he crossed the churchyard and went by the side gate into the garden, where Mrs. Gould was picking narcissus for the altar.

"Good morning, Tony," she said. "You are a very extraordinary shape this morning."

"I know. Can Rose and Dora come back with me, Mrs. Gould?"

Permission was given, and Tony and his companions set off together.

"What have you got in your jersey?" asked Dora.

"Apples, of course. If people will give one rotten bags that burst, one has to put the apples somewhere. My name is Mr. Crabapple," said Tony, sticking his apple-plastered chest out as far as possible and swinging in his walk like a janissary. This exquisite humor amused the little girls so much that it lasted till they reached Mrs. Morland's house. Dora tried once to say that she was Mrs. Crabapple, but receiving no encouragement, she did not again attempt to presume.

When they got back to the house, Tony led the way to the kitchen, where Stoker was washing the floor.

"Here you are, Stokes," he said, pulling his jersey out of his belt. Six very large green apples fell out, and bouncing on the floor rolled away in various corners.

"Now they'll all be bruised," said Stoker. "Why didn't you get Mr. Reid to put them in a bag?"

"I did. If people give one rotten bags that the bottoms fall out of, one can't leave the apples in the road. I thought you wanted them."

"If people took baskets, the same as what their mothers told them, they'd have more sense," said Stoker, whose meaning was abundantly clear, though her form of words left something to be desired.

"Come on, Rose and Dora. I'll read you my essay," said Tony.

"Not till you've picked up them apples," said Stoker. "And I've put all your writing and that rubbish up in the playroom."

His back view stiff with resentment, Tony led his friends upstairs. "Writing and rubbish!" he muttered vengefully.

"You can both sit on the floor," he announced when they reached the play room, taking his seat at the small writing table, "only don't sit too near the station because I've been building a new approach with some empty card boxes and it might fall over. Now I'll read you my essay."

"What's an essay?" asked Dora.

"This is. It's called 'What I would do if I had a hundred pounds.'"

"Oh, I know what I'd do," said Dora. "I'd buy a hundred dogs and take them to Dorland, and build them lovely kennels with huge meadows all around them, and have a dog show and win all the prizes."

Tony stared coldly at her.

"That's not an essay," he said. "And, anyway, you wouldn't, because dogs aren't allowed into Dorland. They have very strict quarantine, and your dogs would have to be in quarantine for seven years, so most of them would be dead by then."

"May I say what I'd do?" asked Rose.

"All right."

Rose went pink and remained silent.

"Well, if you haven't any more ideas than that, you couldn't write an essay," said Tony. "My essay begins, 'One day I was walking along the street when a man stopped me. What will you do he said if I give you a hundred ells?'"

"What are ells?" asked Dora.

"Haven't you ever heard of L s d? The ells are the pounds. L stands for libra and s is for shillings and d for denarius—Latin, if you don't know."

"Daddy said s was for solidus the other day," said Rose, who very unfairly read Latin with her father.

"I know. But that's not an essay, that's only Latin."

"In Dorland the money is called P.S.P," said Dora.

"I know," said Tony, rashly adding, "Why?"

"Pounds, shillings and pence, of course."

Tony flushed darkly, but made a magnificent recovery.

"I know," he said shortly, "but it can't be, because Dorland has a decimal coinage. My essay goes on 'I received this remark cum grano salto and asked where it was.'"

He hurried over this sentence, secretly uneasy lest Rose, the scholar, should take exception to his Latin tag. But Rose had strayed into a world of her own.

"If I had a hundred pounds," she said, her eyes fixed on a visioned world, "I would buy a theater at Rosebush, and Tony could act *As You Like It.*

While she spoke she was toying nervously with the approach to the new station. Without noticing what she was doing she displaced one of the boxes. The station tottered and fell, dragging part of the permanent way to destruction in its fall.

"Oh, Tony, what have I done?" she said, horror struck.

"Simply ruined the railway, that's all. It took me all the holidays up to now to make this railway, and now it is simply ruined. Of course, it's no use my trying to build it up again. When a thing is very good and it gets smashed because people are careless one can't make it again. Never mind," said Tony, for Rose's abject misery began to penetrate even his self-sufficing mind, "we'll have a jolly good accident and smash everything."

With gleaming eyes he began to destroy the permanent way. Dora first, and Rose as she grew bolder, aided in the work of devastation.

"Terrible earthquake at Rosebush," shouted Tony, assuming the role of a newspaper boy. "Thousands dead in the wreckage. Impossible to estimate damage done."

Both little girls screamed with pleasure at the tops of their voices.

"There's an awful earthquake in Dorland, too," said Dora.

"Show it me, then," said Tony, winding up the Windsor Castle with frantic haste and laying it on its side among the ruins where it lay whirring agreeably. "Dorland isn't volcanic; you ought to know that. Look, Stokes," he cried, as that handmaiden opened the door and stood blocking the entrance, "this is the best accident I've ever had."

"I supposes you couldn't all make a bit more noise?" said Stoker, with heavy pleasantry. "Time you young ladies was off, or you'll be late for lunch. Not that it'll spoil by keeping, I dare say."

Gradually the tumult subsided and Rose and Dora went home. After lunch Tony applied himself to editing a Special Railway Accident number of the *Morland Times*, a periodical remarkable chiefly for the rarity of its appearance, the poverty of its material, and the peculiarity of its spelling.

About four o'clock Laura extracted Tony from his editorial labors and cleaned him up for their visit to the Vicarage. Apart from the pleasure of seeing Rose and Dora, whom he saw nearly every day, Tony had little use for formal tea at the Vicarage. Mrs. Gould he considered merely as a provider of food, and as such he tolerated her, but the Vicar and he had little in common. To Tony the Vicar was as trying as Mr. Prothero without the excuse of being a schoolmaster. To ask a chap the aorist of a Greek verb over scones and honey was a betrayal of the rites of hospitality. To the Vicar Tony appeared as that rather forward, spoilt lad of Mrs. Morland's. Of this Laura was fully aware, and though none hated her children more intensely than she when occasion presented, she was quite unable to sympathize with the Vicar's repressive attitude to her youngest son. Teas at the Vicarage therefore were apt to be stiff and embarrassing.

For the beginning of tea Tony behaved and looked like an angel. He passed bread and butter to people who were eating cake, insisted on carrying cups of tea to everyone, slopping it over into the saucers, discussed cricket, which he loathed, with Mrs. Gould, and listened with serenity to the Vicar's very dull account of what he did at Easter.

"You will hardly guess what I did one Saturday, Mrs. Morland," said the Vicar. "I went to the Southbridge Races."

"If you want any racing tips, come to me, sir," said Tony.

"It is very rarely that I go to a race meeting," continued the Vicar, ignoring his young friend, "but Lord Stoke had a horse running."

"I wouldn't back one of his horses, sir," said Tony. "I saw one run last winter and it was absolutely no good at all."

"I think Tony was taken to a race meeting by Mrs. Knox," said Laura nervously, hoping to placate the Vicar by the mention of the good company Tony had been in.

"I had a ripping time, sir," Tony went on, speaking to the Vicar as man to man. "Mrs. Knox wouldn't let me go to the Tote, but I betted with her in halfpennies. I won sevenpence halfpenny. I have studied the form of the horses pretty carefully, and you can take my advice about any races hereabouts. I expect I'd have made about twenty quid if Mrs. Knox had let me go to a bookie. If you go to Southbridge next autumn, sir, mind you take my advice first."

Rose and Dora stared admiringly at their hero in this new role. Mrs. Gould didn't laugh, which did her great credit. The Vicar glared at Tony with a steady disapproving look which had no effect at all.

"I hope," said the Vicar, pointedly addressing Laura, "that you are taking an interest in our harvest festival, Mrs. Morland."

"Of course I am," said Laura, nervous beyond her wont, and trying vainly to make faces at Tony which would stem the flow of his eloquence. "I must send you some flowers, if we have any."

"I hope you'll have some decent hymns, sir," said Tony. "I don't think much of some of the new hymns. I was educated on Ancient and Modern. I've been to heaps of churches, and I don't like those alterations in the service nowadays."

"Oh," said the Vicar, in the accent unkindly associated with our older universities by those who have not attended them, with which he had quelled no less than six choir boys at once at the last annual outing. Laura, recognizing to her horror fragments of her own conversation remodeled by her son, plunged into the fray and told Tony he could go and play in the garden with the girls if Mrs. Gould would excuse them.

"Certainly," said Tony with exquisite courtesy.

He rose, pushed his chair violently back against the Vicar's Sheraton sideboard, offered an arm to each of the girls, and led them to the garden, leaving the dinning room door open. The Vicar then retired to his study and Laura and Mrs. Gould looked at each other.

"We won't disturb the Vicar to say goodbye," said Laura some half hour later. "I feel he might excommunicate Tony if he saw us again."

"He probably would," said his wife comfortingly. "He always excommunicates people on Fridays, on account of his sermon. We'll come out by the garden."

They found the children climbing in an old mulberry tree. Here the thin, long-legged Rose had the advantage, and was perched among the high branches. Tony and Dora were seated in a fork lower down, and Tony was telling the little girls about his experiences as a racing man.

"Of course, you have to go to races quite a lot to get into the know," he said. "I only went once, with Mrs. Knox, when she took me to the Southbridge point-to-point, but I seemed to pick it all up very quickly. I am very friendly with horses, and I have a kind of instinct about them. If you put me in a field with a hundred horses I could easily pick out the winners. *You* couldn't, of course, but you haven't been to a point-to-point like me. Oh, mother, need we go? I was telling Rose and Dora how to pick winners. It will be awfully useful for them when they go to the races."

"They won't be going for a long time," said Mrs. Morland, "so save up your advice. Come down now, Tony; we really must go."

Tony began to climb down. As he jumped from the lowest bough a small branch caught in his blazer pocket and ripped it away from the coat. A quantity of miscellaneous property fell out, including a shabby notebook, three pencils, six large nails, a dog collar and a small dirty paper parcel.

"Pick those up quickly and come along," said Laura. "What do you want a dog's collar for?"

"In case I found a dog, mother, of course. If you met a dog that didn't know where to go you couldn't take it home with you unless it had a collar. Mother, my pocket's all got torn."

"I can see that. Put all that rubbish in your other pocket then. And you've managed to get a three-cornered tear in your knickerbocker leg."

"Here's the you-know-what," said Dora, who was helping to pick up Tony's possessions, as she handed him the paper parcel.

"Right-oh," said Tony. "Remember, nine p.m. tonight."

Rose and Dora nodded mysteriously.

Outside the house Laura paused to say goodbye.

"Goodbye, Mrs. Gould, and thank you very much for a lovely

time," said Tony seraphically, "and if you and Rose and Dora want any racing tips, don't go to the bookies, come to me."

The Vicar's study window was open at the bottom, and Laura could see a pale, indignant face raised from the table where he was working. Panic-stricken, she hurried Tony away.

When they got home she told Tony to take his blazer and knickers off and give them to Stoker to mend. Tony went to the kitchen to tell Stoker about the afternoon's doings.

"I say, Stokes," he began, "my coat and knickers got all torn on the mulberry tree. Please, mother says, will you mend them."

"I should say they did need mending. You might watch out what you do, Master Tony, I haven't nine pairs of hands."

"I know. I can't think why trees have such stupid branches on them. Oh, Stokes, what's that?"

"Macaroni," said Stoker, who was breaking macaroni up into small pieces preparatory to throwing it into a saucepan of boiling water.

"What for?"

"Macaroni cheese. There's that and some castle puddings for your supper."

"Oh, Stoke, don't make the macaroni so small. Put me in some long bits, please."

"All right. Now off you go and tidy that playroom a bit before supper."

When Tony came down to supper his mother wanted to know why he was wearing a dirty pair of running shorts and a dressinggown. Tony's explanation that his knickers and blazer were being mended did not appear to satisfy his mother, who reminded him that he had other knickers, and moreover that he had his best grey flannel suit for evenings and needn't go about looking like a lunatic. With the best grace in the world he went upstairs and came down again with an angel's expression, faultlessly attired.

"Mother, I asked Stokes to put some long bits of macaroni in. Can you find the long bits for me, mother? I rather need them."

Laura hunted about and put some pieces nine or ten inches long on Tony's plate. She then helped herself and filled her glass with water.

When she looked up Tony's head was over his plate and he had the end of a piece of macaroni between his lips. Under her fascinated gaze he drew the long tube into his mouth by suction, rich cheesy sauce dripping from it onto his plate.

"That's the way Italians eat macaroni, mother," he said. "There's a chap at school whose brother went to Italy, and he taught him, and we all did it at lunch when there was macaroni pudding, and matron went off pop. Watch, mother.'"

He repeated the ceremony, and had the giggles in the middle, so that he nearly choked and some of the sauce went on the tablecloth.

"Now, Tony, you are being revolting."

"Oh, mother, I'm not, truly. Just watch me once more."

But he was laughing so much that he couldn't do it, and Laura, against her better nature, had to laugh too.

After supper she sent him to tidy some of the railway accident. Happening to go up about nine o'clock, she found the playroom untouched.

"Where are you, Tony?" she called. "Why didn't you tidy your toys?"

"Mother," came a voice from the bathroom, "I'm just going to bed. I'm cleaning my teeth now. Mother, you know like me to go to bed punctually, and I was finishing my essay. You know you like me to get my essay done."

Laura's eye fell on the essay, which was lying on the table. The author appeared to have made but little progress since the morning.

"—he gided me to a bank where they gave me the mony. So I bought a racehorse and trained it myself and rode it at a point-to-point and won a pot of mony because it had started at a million to one. So then I was so rich that 100£s seemed to me like nothing."

Feeling that there was a want of logic somewhere in Tony's economics, Laura went into the bathroom. Her son had finished cleaning his teeth and gone to his room. The tube of toothpaste, a new one, lay squeezed almost empty on the floor, and the looking glass was decorated with long strips of dentifrice.

"Tony, what have you been doing?" said his exhausted mother.

"How do you mean, mother—doing?" said Tony, rather indistinctly.

"That disgusting, wasteful mess in the bathroom."

"Oh, mother," said Tony, still with impeded articulation, "I was only making macaroni. I had a macaroni factory and then all the toothpaste came out and I couldn't get it in again. You don't like me to dawdle when I'm going to bed, do you?"

A curious smell, not disagreeable in itself, but somehow unsuited to a gentleman's bedroom, assailed Laura's nostrils.

"What are you eating, Tony?" she enquired suspiciously.

"I promised Rose and Dora I'd eat it at nine o'clock, so they could think of me eating it. I wasn't hungry for it after tea, so I just showed it them in the parcel. I said I'd eat it in bed."

"Eat what?"

"The kipper's head, mother, of course. I always eat kippers' heads at school. Mother, do let's do something really interesting tomorrow."

IV

THE CHRISTMAS HOLIDAYS

CHAPTER **I**

CHRISTMAS PRESENTS

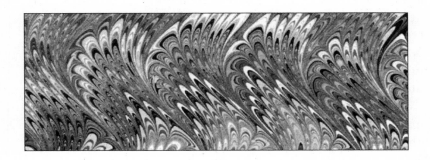

Christmas presents are always a difficulty if one has to buy them out of a shilling a week. A shilling a week sounds a lot, but it is extraordinary how fast it goes. To begin with, one's mother makes one buy one's own stamps out of it, and as one has a good many really important letters to write to the Wade Clockwork Engine Company, and the people who sell picture postcards of all the types of English railway engines, it eats up one's income. Then one must have blue ink and red ink and green ink to draw pictures with, and a grindstone and some oil and a coarse whetstone and a fine whetstone and a leather strop, if one wants to keep one's scout's sheath knife in good condition. Even if you get them at Woolworth's all these things mount up.

Therefore Tony, counting up his money on the twenty-third of December, the day after school had broken up, found that all he could spare for Christmas presents was two shillings and elevenpence halfpenny. Out of this he wanted to get presents for his mother, Stoker, Rose and Dora, Dr. Ford, Mrs. Mallow, Mr. Mallow, Sid Brown, Mr. Brown at the garage, Mr. Reid at the general store, Adrian Coates and his wife and baby, Mr. and Mrs. Knox, and Sylvia, his headmaster's wife's golden cocker spaniel.

It was true that he could count on a good Christmas tip from Mr. Coates and Mr. Knox, and very likely something from his mother and

Dr. Ford, but unfortunately these contributions to his exchecker would not be available till Christmas Day. If people knew that one needed money to buy Christmas presents with, thought Tony, they ought to give it one a bit earlier; say, as soon as the holidays began. On the other hand, even if they did give one the money, one really needed it oneself to buy a new clockwork engine, the present locomotive, the four-six-nought Windsor Castle, being unequal to hauling the coal truck, the four corridor coaches, the goods truck, milk van, and brake van which constituted Tony's rolling stock.

He began to reckon up what he might with luck get in the way of tips. Mr. Coates was usually good for a pound if he saw one, but otherwise he mightn't remember. One must ask mother if he was likely to be staying with Mr. Knox for Christmas. Mr. Knox was also good for a pound, and as he was having a large tea party on Christmas Eve that was pretty safe. Mother sometimes gave one ten shillings and sometimes a present. If the present was already bought, it was too late to do anything. One must try to find out, and if possible guide her thoughts towards a pecuniary contribution. His elder brothers generally sent a money order, varying from five shillings to a pound, according to the state of their finances. If Dr. Ford were at Mr. Knox's tea party he might give one a half-a-crown or even five shillings.

All this uncertainty was very trying for a person. If one knew that one could count on about six pounds, one could get the engine and some more rails. If, on the other hand, it was only going to be two pounds ten, or three pounds, one would have to put it in the bank and wait till one got some more. There really ought to be two Christmases; one about the twenty-second of December for people to get their tips and another on the ordinary day for them to get their presents. Then one would know where one was.

Tony chose a key from a large bunch which was chained to him, and locked his little black japanned cash box with a sigh. This bunch of keys was one of the many sources of contention between its owner and the school matron. It consisted of his school locker key, the key of his cash box, trunk and bag, one large key known to open the school boot-hole—a secret jealously guarded by Tony and his friend Master

Wesendonck—a key which once unlocked a padlock that Tony had lost, the key which had opened Master Wesendonck's father's garage before the lock was changed, and seven other keys which opened nothing. Matron's contention was that those keys did nothing but wear holes in Morland's pockets. Tony upheld the usefulness of keys in general, and in particular of keys with no known locks, as there was always a chance that they might open something they weren't meant to open. In this theory he had been justified on the incredibly lucky occasion when he and Master Wesendonck were convalescing in the sanatorium after chickenpox, and found that one of the keys opened the little door which led from the sanatorium garden into the playground. At the door they were able to hold court, surrounded by a number of admiring friends who exchanged toys and school magazines with them and listened with envy to their untruthful accounts of the luxuries of sanatorium diet. Matron, seeing the crowd from an upper window, had come hurrying to the spot, slammed the door, driven Tony and Master Wesendonck back to their bedroom, and burnt all the magazines. No one else caught chickenpox, a fact which matron, with complete want of logic, attributed to her confiscation of the toys and papers. Matron never discovered how the door had been opened, so it all proved how one ought to keep every key that one finds.

Tony climbed over the banisters and came down on the outside of the staircase, as he had often been forbidden to do. His mother was already sitting at breakfast, so he pushed his face against her ear and sat down.

"Mother," he said, "what do you want for Christmas?"

Laura Morland never failed to be touched by this question, and answered as usual that she really didn't want anything.

"Oh, but, mother, you must. You can't not have a present."

"It's perfectly darling of you, Tony, but honestly, old mothers don't want presents. Will you draw me a picture for Christmas?"

"Oh, mother! A picture's not a present. I want to get you something real. Mother, do you suppose you are likely to give me some money at

Christmas, or would it be more economical for you to give me a present?"

"Which would you like?"

"Well, mother, I think money would really be more convenient, if you can really afford it. I mean one can buy things with it. Have you any idea, mother, about how much it would be?"

"I should think it might be ten shillings, Tony."

"Oh, mother, good on you. Mother, if you can afford it, do you think I could have it before Christmas, because I could use it to buy Christmas presents. I want to buy a saucepan for Sibyl's baby. I thought a saucepan would be a very nice present. You can get jolly good saucepans for sixpence at Woolworth's, and it would be very useful for cooking things in. Matron used to make cocoa and hot milk for us in the san. with a saucepan. What do you think, mother?"

"Isn't Sibyl's baby a little young for a saucepan, Tony? After all, it is only six months old. Wouldn't a soft toy be better?"

"But that wouldn't be a real present, mother. A saucepan would be so useful."

Laura abandoned the unequal contest and told Tony to be ready at eleven o'clock to drive to Southbridge, where the nearest Woolworth was. At the Vicarage they picked up Rose and Dora, who also had Christmas shopping to do.

"How much have you got to spend?" asked Tony, when they had started. "I've got ten shillings, and two and elevenpence halfpenny. I've got to get sixteen presents with it. It will be a bit difficult, but I am very good at Christmas presents. I don't know how it is, but I always seem to be able to get presents very cheaply and they are very nice ones. I suppose I have a kind of gift for getting presents."

"We have got five shillings each," said Rose.

"How miserable," said Tony. "Never mind, I'll help you. If you are in difficulties come to me and I'll give you advice. I'm going to get a saucepan for Sibyl's baby."

"A toy saucepan?" asked Dora.

"Of course not. A real saucepan to cook milk and things in. It will be very useful. Just because one is a baby one doesn't need idiotic toys.

It is much better to have something that will come in useful when one is bigger."

When they got to Southbridge Laura parked her car. She then opened her bag and gave Tony a ten-shilling note.

"Here you are, Tony, with my love," she said.

"Oh, thanks awfully, mother. Mother, what do you want me to get you?"

"Nothing, darling, really."

"Oh, but mother, you must."

He pulled a very shabby purse out of his pocket and opened it upside down. A clinking shower of small silver and pennies fell into the road. The little girls came to the rescue and helped to pick them up.

"Here, mother," said Tony, red in the face from his exertions in extricating a halfpenny from its hiding place under a stationary motor coach. "I did mean to give you sixpence to spend on yourself, but I can only manage a threepenny bit and twopence halfpenny. Do you mind? If you saw something you wanted for sixpence, perhaps you could spend another halfpenny yourself and then I could pay you back out of my next pocket money. Come on, mother."

"Wait a minute," said Laura, still hunting about in her bag. "Here, Rose, here is half-a-crown for you and one for Dora, to help with Christmas presents."

"Oh, thank you, Mrs. Morland," said the little girls rapturously.

The party entered Woolworth's, which was seething as usual with anxious mothers grasping their baskets and their babies, girls looking for necklaces, earrings, lipstick and rouge, well-to-do ladies buying cups and saucers and plates by the dozen for their village festivities, working men buying rubber heels and leather soles to repair the family boots, children clutching hardly-saved sixpences, children with no sixpences enjoying the glittering counters, dozens of dogs on leads winding themselves around people's legs and uttering yelps of distress. Behind the counter Mr. Woolworth's young ladies were serving one customer, telling another where the handkerchief counter was, rapping on the cash register to attract the superintendent, who alone had power to get change for a pound note, managing to carry on long conversations with each other as they served, and on the whole keeping their heads surprisingly.

"Rose and Dora," said Mrs. Morland, "you had better stick to me. Tony, you can do your own shopping and meet us at the weighing machine when you are ready."

Tony had got his purse out again and extracted a shilling.

"I can't bother to find presents for you and Rose," he said to Dora, "so here is a shilling for you both. That's sixpence each."

Without waiting for thanks he strode off towards the kitchen section to inspect saucepans. The array of aluminum was dazzling and Tony's determination to buy a saucepan began to waver. After all, Sibyl's baby, if it had any sense, would like a shining mug just as much, or there was a glittering plate, and a small jug, and a nutmeg grater, and basting spoons, and collapsible cups, any one of which a sensible baby should be proud to possess. Unable to make up his mind, Tony strolled along the counters till his attention was caught by a tray of dog collars—red, blue, green and brown. Exactly what darling Sylvia, his headmaster's wife's golden cocker spaniel, would like.

Such was the press of grown-ups that Tony's smaller form remained unnoticed for some time. At the last the girl behind the counter was able to give him her attention.

"Which should you think was a good sort of collar for a golden cocker?" asked Tony.

"Eh?" said the girl, adding to a friend, "so I said eight o'clock or not at all."

"Serve him right," said the friend.

"Which sort of collar should you think would be right for a golden cocker spaniel?" asked Tony again.

"Collars are all in the tray over there," said the girl, "and that's what I told his mother."

"You didn't!" said the friend admiringly.

"But which one do you think would be best for a golden cocker called Sylvia?" said Tony again.

"Eh? Well, there's a nice red, and a green and a blue. I don't suppose she'll speak to me again in a hurry."

"That's right," said the friend, wrapping up parcels for two customers and giving correct change without looking.

A little dashed by not getting the attention to which he was accustomed, Tony examined the collars. Darling Sylvia would like a red collar, he thought. She had a brown one already, so a red one would be a change.

"Could I have this red one?" he asked, holding it up.

By this time the girl was serving another customer and paid no attention to him.

"Of course, if people don't want to sell things they needn't," said Tony aloud to himself, though rather inclined to tears at being so neglected. But just then his eye was caught by a tray of rubber toys for dogs. A large grey rubber bone would be far better than a collar. After all, Sylvia had a collar already and a hard rubber ball, but a bone would be something new. With great care he chose the best bone he could find, meticulously examining the whole heap before making his final choice. Holding the bone and his ten shilling note toward the assistant, he said in the voice with which he had so successfully declaimed the part of Adam in the school production of *As You Like It*, "I want this bone, please, and here is a ten shilling note."

Even the lion-house clamor of Woolworth's was stilled for a moment in his immediate neighborhood.

"What's that?" said the assistant.

"I want this sixpenny bone, please," said Tony, in the same fine resonant voice.

"Can't serve everyone at once," snapped the girl, putting two pencil sharpeners and a leatherette notebook into a bag.

A chorus of protest immediately arose on Tony's behalf. A man in a shabby overcoat said he was in no hurry. A girl with a dirty white crochet cap worn on one ear said it was a shame not to attend to the kid. Several women asked Tony if the bone was for his own doggie. The owner of a Pekingese unplaited it from her neighbor's feet, held it up, and asked it if it wouldn't like a nice bony-wony like the one the nice little boy was buying for his doggy-woggy. The assistant bowed to the pressure of public opinion, took Tony's note, gave him his change, put a bone in a bag and shoved it at him.

"Thank you," said Tony. "Sylvia is a darling dog and she will simply love the bone. When she came to stay with us one summer——"

But by this time the fickle attention of the crowd had been transferred to a quarrel between the other assistant and a young girl who, being of the same age and class, had no inhibitions about saying what she thought of people who seemed to be paid for standing behind a counter doing nothing when other people were in a hurry.

Tony took a small notebook out of his pocket, opened it at a list of people to whom he wanted to give presents, found a stub of pencil and put a cross against the name Sylvia. There were still fifteen presents to buy, and the present for Sibyl's baby was undecided. For friends in the village cards or calendars seemed an easy solution of the Christmas problem. Tony looked earnestly at his list. Stoker, Mr. Mallow, Sid Brown, Mr. Brown, Mr. Reid, Mrs. Mallow would all have to be content with cards. After all, if one only has ten shillings—at least nine and sixpence it is now—and two and elevenpence half-penny—at least it is only one and sixpence, since one gave one's mother fivepence halfpenny and Rose and Dora a shilling between them, one must economize a bit. Six exquisite cards of puppies and kittens, forget-me-nots, holly and robins, coaching scenes, Tower Bridge, and a lady and gentleman dancing a minuet were only threepence each. These purchases made, Tony felt more at liberty to concentrate on his other friends, especially on Mr. Coates, who was really an understanding sort of person and could help one with one's Ovid in case of need, besides having an airplane of his own in which one's mother wouldn't let one go. But Tony, though he had never heard of the word attrition, had great faith in his own powers of wearing down his mother's resistance. He had found by long experience that if one asked for a thing often enough, simply ignoring rebuffs and refusals, one could usually get what one wanted. In the matter of the airplane his mother had been adamant, but Tony was not at all discouraged, and had visions of himself flying high in the air, preferably over his school, and boasting to all his friends about it afterwards. Perhaps for Mr. Coates something for his airplane would be useful. Tony wandered about among the counters till a tray of motor goggles caught his eye. Undoubtedly just the sort of thing Mr. Coates would want. Just as his purchase, price sixpence, was being handed to him, his mother and Rose and Dora came up.

"Hello, mother," said Tony, "I've spent three and elevenpence halfpenny, concluding what I gave to you and Rose and Dora, so I have nine shillings left. I shall keep seven shillings to put in the bank and spend two shillings more."

"Are you nearly ready, Tony?" said his mother.

"Oh, mother! I've still got to get presents for Sibyl and Dr. Ford and Mr. and Mrs. Knox. Oh, mother, what have you got for my present for you?"

"I got a photograph frame to put that snapshot of Gerald in that he sent from Tibet."

"Did it cost sixpence?"

"Yes."

"That's all right. Next time you give me my pocket money, give me a halfpenny too little. What did Rose and Dora get?"

"I got a lovely brooch," said Rose, displaying a piece of sham mosaic with a flower on it.

"That's only threepence," said Tony. "I saw them on the counter."

"Well, I let Dora have the other threepence," said Rose humbly, "because she really needed it."

"You see," said Dora, a little uneasy under Tony's piercing glance, "I got a lovely golden box for my sixpence, and then I hadn't anything to put in it, so Rose gave me threepence to buy some sweets. Have one?"

"No thanks," said Tony, taking out his purse. "Here, Rose, here's sixpence for you so that you can buy as much as Dora. I did rather need that sixpence myself, but it doesn't matter."

"Oh, Tony, really I don't need it."

"Take it, take it," said Tony loftily, pressing it into her hand.

"Don't be long now," said his mother, who had been buying strings of colored glass ornaments for the Vicarage Christmas tree. "We shall be waiting for you at the weighing machine."

Tony continued his perambulations, trying to decide upon the best way of spending the one and sixpence which remained from the sum he had allotted to his shopping. For Dr. Ford a threepenny napkin ring seemed to meet the occasion. For Sibyl he bought a glass brooch in the shape of the letter C. He wanted an S, but they were out of S's. Even so the C bore an uneasy resemblance to a G, but Sibyl would understand, and it was so beautiful that it was well worth sixpence. As Mr. Knox wrote books, a threepenny red pencil that you screwed in and out seemed suitable. For Mrs. Knox he found a threepenny handkerchief with a lace edge and a bouquet of roses embroidered in the corner, and still had three pennies left.

With the sensation of being a benefactor to the human race, Tony made his way towards the weighing machine. A penny spent in getting his weight, which also included his fortune, would not be a bad investment. He put all his parcels on the floor, stood on the machine and put in his penny. A card emerged from a metal slot. "You will be prosperous in all undertakings commenced on a Friday," he read. "You are sensitive and have many gifts. Do not be easily discouraged. Good luck will await you when you least expect it."

At this moment his mother and the girls joined him.

"Are you ready, Tony?" said his mother.

"Ready for ages," said Tony, picking up his parcels. As they got into a car Tony emitted a groan.

"Oh, mother, I've forgotten the saucepan for Sibyl's baby."

"You would," said his mother. "Well, run back and get it quickly, or we'll all be late for lunch."

"But, mother, I've spent all the money."

"All my ten shillings and your money too?"

"Well, practically. At least you see, mother, I promised myself I'd put seven shillings in the bank for my railway, because it really needs it, so I only have twopence left."

"Here's my sixpence," said Rose, holding out the coin that Tony had given her. "I didn't spend it and I really don't want it."

"It is yours," said Tony magnificently.

"No, you have it."

"Oh, all right. Thanks most awfully."

Much relieved, he scurried off and returned before long with the saucepan in a paper bag.

"I got my fortune in the weighing machine," he announced to the little girls as they drove home. "It said I had lots of gifts. That was pretty good, wasn't it? I suppose I have more parcels than anyone. I don't know why, but somehow I seem to be very generous about presents. And it said I'd have good luck and that was true, because if I hadn't given you that sixpence, Rose, I wouldn't have been able to buy the saucepan for Sibyl's baby. I expect it will be terribly pleased to have a saucepan. What is its name, mother?"

"Laura."

"But, mother, that is your name."

"I know it is."

"Then why did they call it that?"

"After me."

"It seems rather silly to call a baby after you," said Tony. "You're not even its mother. I shall call it Arual."

"Why?" asked the little girls.

"Laura backwards, if you could spell, or had any sense," said Tony briefly.

He and Dora then played a rather dull game of saying everyone's name backwards. Ynot, Arod and Esor sent them into fits of giggles, while Rekots seemed to be the wittiest thing that had ever happened. Rose took no part in the game, sitting silent in a corner, looking out of the window, and as she was usually much quieter than Dora, no one noticed her. When they got to the Vicarage Laura got out to speak to Mrs. Gould for a moment. Dora and Tony were still giggling over their game, but Rose got out quickly and hurried towards the house. Something about her made Laura feel anxious, and she called to her. Rose turned obediently and came back. She was a pitiful sight, her nose shiny, her face blotched, her eyes still streaming with tears.

"What on earth is the matter?" asked Laura with real concern, sitting down on the running board and taking Rose's lanky little form into her arms.

Rose only burrowed her head into Laura's shoulder and shook with uncontrollable sobs. Tony and Dora stopped giggling and looked on, wide-eyed and rather uncomfortable.

"What is it, darling?" said Laura again. "Take my handkerchief and wipe your eyes."

Rose, always docile, blew her nose and sat on Laura's lap, looking the picture of woebegone misery.

"Tony and Dora haven't been teasing you, have they?" asked Laura, who was not unaware that the two younger and more turbulent spirits sometimes banded together against the older and gentler Rose.

Rose shook her head a great many times.

"Do you feel ill?" said Laura, pursuing her enquiries.

"No, it's not that," sobbed Rose in a choked voice. "It's my sixpence. I did want Tony to have it, but I did want it so much myself, Mrs. Morland, and I couldn't help crying when I thought of it."

Overcome with the misery of self-sacrifice, she relapsed into tears again, while Laura sat hugging and soothing her, and looking at Tony to see whether he would rise to the occasion.

Tony went very pink. Nobility and avarice were obviously struggling in his soul, and his mouth twitched with conflicting emotions. Suddenly he dashed around to the other side of the car, and returned with a parcel, which he pushed at Rose.

"I can't exactly spare that sixpence, Rose," he said, "because my railway really needs it, but if you like you can have the saucepan."

Rose's sobs ceased as if by magic. Her eyes begin to shine, and a watery but satisfied smile overspread her tear stained face.

"Oh, Tony, can I really have it for my own?"

"Of course you can. It's a jolly good saucepan and probably worth about a shilling really. You can cook all sorts of things in it."

"Thank you ever so much," said Rose, clasping the saucepan ecstatically in her arms. "You are so kind. I'm glad I gave you my sixpence."

"And what about Sibyl's baby?" asked Laura, getting up and tidying herself from the effects of Rose's damp abandonment.

"Well, mother," said Tony, "I should have thought you would know that saucepans aren't really much good for babies. Besides, Sibyl's baby is quite small, and I don't suppose it has even heard of Christmas. If it wants a present I'll give it one of my old tin railway carriages that I don't use now. Mother, what is there for lunch?"

CHAPTER 2

FAREWELL, MORLAND

It was the last day of the Christmas holidays. Tony looked forward to the next term with interest and a slight sinking of the heart. He was going into the upper school. Five years spent in the lower school had made him a well-known character, and he realized, with little enthusiasm, that he would now have to start all over again. Master Wesendonck would be moving up with him, but owing to an unfair knack of doing maths rather well he would be on the science side, while Tony would be on what has unfortunately come to be the refuge of the mediocre, the classical side. His other special friend, Fair-weather, would alas be left behind, as even his brilliant athletic record could not get him through his examinations, though all the masters did their best.

All this was a bit depressing for a chap, and though his excellent appetite was undiminished and he was capable of sleeping till nine o'clock if not pulled out of bed, his spirits were not quite their usual selves. From time to time, and always when his mother happened to be about, a gentle settled melancholy fell upon him. He occasionally alluded in her presence to his coming trial with a fine blend of self-pity and resignation, while kindly making it clear to her that it was not actually her fault.

"It's pretty rotten being at the big school, mother," he said. "You have to do an awful lot of prep and the lights are so bad that most of the boys are practically blind."

"Tony, I can't believe that. After all, Gerald and John were both in the Upper School and neither of them is blind."

"I know," said Tony, who rather resented any comparisons between himself and his elder brothers, "but I expect the lights were better then, and, anyway, Gerald wears spectacles, mother. I expect I'll have to wear spectacles when I go to the upper school. There was a chap in the upper school who wore spectacles, and he was playing cricket, and a ball smashed his spectacles right into his eyes, so that he was blind, too. I wish I wasn't going into Mr. Holland's house, mother. There was a chap in his house that has a brother at school, and the brother said this chap had meat to eat that was full of tubes, so he couldn't eat it and he got appendicitis."

"Did the brother tell you that himself?" asked Laura, accustomed by long use to discount heavily anything that her sons told her about the horrors of school.

"Not exactly, mother."

"Who did then?"

"Well, mother, you wouldn't understand, but there was a chap called Swift-Hetherington who knew the brother, and he used to tell us all about it in the dorm, after lights out. It's all absolutely true, mother."

"I dare say," said Laura, who was on her knees wrestling with Tony's packing. "If you have meat with tubes let me know and I'll send you a pork pie and a cake."

"Oh, mother! I couldn't possibly have a pork pie at school. The chaps would give me no end of a time."

"All right, then don't grumble," said Laura, who was secretly anxious and unhappy at the thought of her youngest son going a step further into a cold world. In spite of the happy and normal careers of her three elder sons she still felt, unreasonably, as she knew, with a mind colored by early readings of *Tom Brown's School Days* and *The Crofton Boys*, that the upper school was a cross between the Inquisition and an unreformed Newgate. Much as she wished Tony's self-esteem to be lowered a peg or two, she dreaded the thought of the process and would probably worry for many nights to come over a vision of a cowed or humiliated little boy, too proud and reticent to tell his wrongs. The stories of the blind boys and the meat with tubes, though reason and experience forbade her to attach any importance to them, would also haunt her wakeful hours in the dark nights. Reticent herself, preferring to wear out her heart and spirits in silence when life was hard, she rarely allowed herself the luxury of discussing her anxieties and obtaining the relief that an outpouring of complaints can bring. When Anne Todd had been her secretary she used sometimes to talk to her, but Anne Todd was now Anne Knox, and though the affection was always there, Anne had other interests. To Adrian she might have spoken, but a sound instinct told her that to make demands on a man's sympathy is not the best way to keep his friendship, so she refrained. Also Adrian had now his wife and baby, which altered, though it in no way spoiled, their relationship.

It is vain to look into the future, but probably Laura's fears for Tony were even more groundless than her many other self-tormentings. The Tonys of this world are well armed against its buffets.

"Five pairs of socks, and one being washed, and your football stockings. And what about handkerchiefs?" said Laura, distractedly making hay in a large pile of clothes on the ground. "You ought to have eighteen, though why so many when you never use more than one a month unless I make you, I can't tell. Bother! I can only find thirteen here. Tony, where are the others? Empty your pockets."

With an evil grace Tony pulled two very unpleasant handkerchiefs out of his knickerbocker pockets.

"That's fifteen," said Laura, "and Stoker must wash those two. Oh, Stoker," she added, as her handmaiden came in with a pile of freshly ironed shirts and collars, "please wash these handkerchiefs out at once. And have you any more?"

"There's one clean one here," said Stoker, "as clean as boiling can make it, though that's not saying much, after the way Master Tony was using it for his paints."

"That's still only sixteen," said Laura, whose hair was by now quite beyond her control. "Tony do *think*."

"Well, mother, there's the one Stokes took away from me the day I brought the toad home in it."

"And quite right too," said Stoker. "Nasty spiteful creatures, them toads."

"Oh, Stokes, they're not. This was a very nice toad, and I was carrying him home because he was too tired to walk. Stokes, if you were a toad and too tired to walk, you would be very pleased if someone took you home in their handkerchief."

"Well, being as I'm not a toad nor likely to be one," said Stoker, "there's no saying. But I won't have no toads in *my* kitchen, Master Tony. That handkerchief gone straight in the kitchen fire, and the best place for it."

"Then that's still sixteen," said Laura. "Oh, my goodness, I shall never get this packing done, and we have to go to tea at Low Rising. What's all this, Tony?"

Her son was surreptitiously pushing into a corner of his school trunk an untidy paper parcel. Laura took it out and undid it. Inside it were a bottle of Butygloss Hair Fixative, a tin of Floral Solidified Brilliantine, and an indefinable grey lump of dirt.

"What is that, Tony?" said his mother, holding up the lump with great distaste.

"That, mother? Oh, *that*. It's only some putty, mother. I got it when the men were mending the Vicarage sink yesterday, and I'm taking it back to school, because it will be very useful."

"Well, it won't," said his exasperated mother. "It's as hard as a stone now. Throw it away."

"Oh, mother! It only needs some linseed oil, and it would be perfectly useful again. Oh, mother!"

"Give it here," said Stoker, taking the lump from her mistress's hands. "Where do you think you're going to get linseed oil at school, Master Tony? Castor oil, more likely. And here's my lord's handkerchief."

With triumph she unwound from the putty the remains of Tony's seventeenth handkerchief and held it up for inspection.

"That one'll have to go the same way as the one the toad was in," she said. "And I'll wash out the other two, and now you leave your poor mother alone, Master Tony, and come and help me do the vegetables for supper. You go and get a good lay down before you go out, it'll do you good," she threw over her shoulder at Laura. "And don't you go worrying over Master Tony's packing; I'll see to it. You'll only go counting them handkercheeves till you get the brain fever, likely as not."

She went out with Tony, slamming the door.

Left alone, Laura finished packing the rest of Tony's shirts and his touchingly small collars. The hair preparations she left on the dressing table for Tony to pack in his first-night bag, if he felt equal to braving the possible disapproval of his new matron. Then she went to her own room, where Stoker had already put a hot-water bottle on the sofa and composed herself for the lay down advocated by that thoughtful woman. But not even the excellent thriller, "The Howling Horror," which she had borrowed from Dr. Ford, could wholly dull in her mind the gnawing ache of fear for Tony's first term as an upper school boy.

Meanwhile Tony and Stoker were doing the vegetables. That is, Stoker did the work while Tony perused the Sunday paper which was Stoker's sole reading.

"I say, Stokes," said Tony, "what do you think about Hitler?"

"No call to think about him at all as far as I can see," said Stoker. "He leaves me alone and I leave him alone. See?"

"Yes, but Stokes, how would you like it if you were a German and Hitler came and murdered you?"

"Stands to reason he wouldn't do no such thing," said Stoker, who brought to bear on all public questions a robust common sense that Dr. Johnson might have envied. "It's not likely I'd go being a German at my time of life."

"I know. But Stokes, supposing you were a German, what would you do? I know what I'd do. I'd put an electric shock machine in the telephone, and then when Hitler answered the telephone he'd get electrocuted. Do you know, Stokes, practically everyone in Germany gets murdered?"

"Serves them right," said Stoker, without specifying any reason for this vengeful remark. "I always said we'd never get no peace till the Kaiser was dead, and now look at them. You go and get clean now, Master Tony. Your mother'll be wanting you to go over to them Knoxes."

At four o'clock Laura, feeling as one usually does all the worse for her lay down, staggered from her sofa and called Tony to come and get ready. At her first call her son appeared, miraculously clean and tidy in his dark blue suit with trousers, his hair well slabbed down, and one corner of a white handkerchief sticking triangularly out of his breast pocket.

"Oh, there's the eighteenth handkerchief," said Laura. "At least it's only the sixteenth now, as Stoker has burnt the toad one and the putty one. I'll have to get you some more and post them to you at school. Get your coat, Tony; we must be going now."

"Oh, mother, need I wear a coat? People won't be able to see my trousers properly if I wear a coat."

"Yes, you need. It's bitterly cold now and it will be colder coming back. We'll have to walk, because the car is down at the garage and won't be ready till tomorrow morning. And get your muffler."

"My muffler? Oh, mother, must I?"

Tony unwillingly put on his coat and muffler. He compromised on the coat by leaving it open so that as many people as possible in the village should see his trousers. Unfortunately it was early closing day, and the bitter cold kept everyone at home who was not forced to go out, so the village street was empty. Tony found that when he had, as a matter of principle, shown resentment by walking a yard behind his mother and groaning when told to come on, he was glad enough to button his overcoat and burrow his chin into his muffler. It was almost dark when they got to Low Rising, and the big fire in the sitting room was a welcome sight. Anne Knox greeted Laura affectionately.

"Welcome, welcome, dear Laura," said George Knox. "You will find yourself among friends here. Sibyl and Adrian are still with us, and the Goulds are all coming, and Ford, and possibly Lord Stoke. Never, Laura, am I so happy as when surrounded by my friends."

"Old English Squire Dispensing Hospitality to Dependants," said Laura, rather tartly, for her mind was still heavy with the thought of Tony's departure.

"Laura, you are unjust," said George Knox. "You ascribe to me sentiments which are foreign to my nature. All I ask is light and warmth and the voices of friends. There is, I hope, no hint of patronage in this. Warmth, whether physical or moral, is all I crave, no unreasonable request."

"Sorry, George," said Laura, "I'm rather cross today. But as for warmth, there's nothing like human breath for warming a place up, and if we are going to sit down thirteen to tea, which is what it looks like, and a fire halfway up the chimney, you will certainly be warm enough, even without wearing all those waistcoats."

"Thirteen?" said George Knox, greatly alarmed. "Good God, Laura! What do you say?"

"You needn't mind that, sir," said Tony. "I'm not supersistious and I don't mind at all."

"No one cares whether you mind or not, my boy," said George Knox. "It is your elders that I am considering. If we sit down thirteen, whoever first rises from the table is doomed, in popular credence, and that we cannot altogether ignore, founded as it is on immemorial and in many cases very unpleasant traditions and rites, doomed, I say, to die within the year."

"Then you'd better ask Lord Stoke to get up first, sir," said Tony. "He's pretty old already, so I dare say it wouldn't really matter. Besides, you don't die unless you are supersistious. I wouldn't die, for instance. I don't suppose the Vicar would die either."

"It might be worth trying," said Anne Knox, who was, we hope, alluding to her spiritual adviser.

"Oh, Laura," she continued, "I want to ask you something quickly before the Goulds come. Do you think that the Vicar will want to say grace? Of course, if it would give him any pleasure I'll willingly ask him, and, of course, if it was dinner, or even lunch, there would be no doubt about it, but do you think tea counts as a meal from a religious point of view? George is so unhelpful about it."

"I don't quite know," said Laura, seriously considering. "Tea isn't usually a real meal, though your teas, Anne, are different. Yes, I think as the Vicar is High Church you needn't worry about it. If he were Low Church I somehow feel that tea would be more important in his life."

Upon this the Vicarage party came in and Adrian and Sibyl appeared.

"We have all come," said Mrs. Gould to Anne. "You said all, Mrs. Knox, so I thought you wouldn't mind if Ruth and Sylvia came too. I hope six isn't too many."

"It's a jolly good thing you did all come," said Tony to Dora. "Some people were getting supersistious about us being thirteen, and now Ruth has come we'll be fourteen, so they can jolly well stop being supersistious. Do you notice anything special about me? Rose, do you?"

"No," said both the little girls with one breath.

"I suppose you don't know the difference between trousers and knickerbockers then," said Tony, turning away from them scornfully.

As Lord Stoke had now arrived, they all sat down to tea around the big table. Anne did homage to the conventions by having Lord Stoke and the Vicar one on each side of her. Dora got next to Tony, while Rose took shelter between Sibyl, who was always kind, and George Knox, who could be relied upon to ignore her, especially as he had Sylvia on his other side. Laura found herself between Adrian and the not very interesting Ruth Gould, who ran a chicken farm with a friend on the other side of Southbridge.

"And how is your little boy, Mrs. Coates?" said the Vicar to Sibyl.

"Well, really, as a matter of fact she is a girl," said Sibyl apologetically, "but she's frightfully well, thank you."

"Oh, sir," said Tony from the opposite side of the table, "had you forgotten Sibyl's baby was a girl? She's been a girl ever since she was born. I should have thought you would have remembered that, sir.

When I grow up I shan't have any girls. Girls are a nuisance. I shall have two boys and call them Stoker and Robert."

The Vicar, never an admirer of Tony's, looked unfavorably at him and turned in a marked way to his hostess.

"Well, I shall call them Frogs and Snails," said Dora, never backward in the fray. "And if you have any more boys I'll call them Puppy Dogs' Tails, so there."

"And if anyone can be bothered to marry *you*, which I don't suppose they will," said Tony in a loud voice, "you'll have a lot of stupid girls, and I'll call them Sugar and Spice and Mice and Lice."

At this very unsuitable parody of well-known lines, Dora, Rose and Adrian began to laugh. The Vicar glared. Laura angrily poked Adrian with her elbow.

"Adrian, don't encourage Tony," she said. "He's all above himself on account of wearing his trousers and going to the upper school. I have troubles enough without you turning my child against me," she added, looking at Adrian with a reproachful gaze.

Adrian was too much overcome by the injustice of this accusation to defend himself.

"Adrian, you were at a public school," continued Laura, as if this were a rare and difficult feat. "Do you think Tony will be miserable and have his spirit broken? I know I'm very silly, but I can't help thinking about it at night. He is really more understanding and sensitive than you would think, and it would be so awful to think of him being cowed."

Adrian was just going to assure Laura, as kindly as possible, that it was, on the whole, Tony's masters and schoolfellows who were to be pitied, when the resonant voice of the sensitive child was heard to address the table.

"Mr. Knox," it said, overcrowing all other conversation, "did you notice that we are thirteen people at tea after all? That's because Ruth came. If Ruth hadn't come, there would be twelve people. I bet if anyone is supersistious they are feeling jolly uncomfortable now. I wonder which of us will die first, don't you, sir?"

"I should think you would, Tony, if your friends' wishes could do anything in the matter," said Dr. Ford, who had come quietly in. "You shut up and eat your tea, and make some room for me. Then we shall be fourteen."

Dr. Ford pulled up a chair and pushed himself in unceremoniously next to Tony, a position which curiously enough was also next to Sylvia Gould. Under cover of a hubbub which had broken out between George Knox and the Vicar about the probable date of a carving in the ruins of Rising Castle, the views of the owner himself being entirely ignored by both parties, Dr. Ford was able to ask Sylvia when she started her new job.

"Next week," said Sylvia. "It will be such fun to teach in a school in Switzerland. I've always wanted to go there."

"I never have till now," said Dr. Ford with intense meaning.

Sylvia looked at him with calm interest, but said nothing.

"I wish to God you weren't going," said Dr. Ford, cutting himself a large slice of bread from the loaf and plastering it with butter and jam. "You'll probably marry a foreigner."

"Why? All right, Tony, there's a piece of bread for you."

"Because I don't want you to. Oh, all *right*, Tony, there's the jam."

"Why not?" said Sylvia.

"Dr. Ford," Laura called across the table, "the Horror didn't howl at all, after all. It was only called the Howling Horror because it lived in a village called Howling. Most unfair. But thank you for lending it to me all the same."

"It's a jolly decent book, sir," said Tony. "The Horror was a man who was all deformed because he had shell shock, and his jaw was all eaten away. Wouldn't it be a good idea to act it after tea, mother? I'll be the Horror and I'll frighten everyone. I bet Annie and cook will be frightened when they see me with my jaw all eaten away. Dr. Ford, if a person had their jaw all eaten away——"

"Shut up," said Dr. Ford.

The argument between George Knox and the Vicar, momentarily interrupted by Laura's remarks, now rose higher than ever, which enabled Dr. Ford to go on with whatever it was that he was trying to say to Sylvia.

"Sylvia," said he, "I feel that a girl like you who can suppress Tony Morland would be wasted on Switzerland. You couldn't consider a position as a village doctor's assistant, could you?"

"What are you offering?"

"Everything I have got," said Dr. Ford with sudden violence.

"Sylvia," said Mrs. Gould from the other side of the table, "what are Tony and Dora doing?"

The two reprobates in question were showing each other something which was concealed on their laps, and were helpless with giggles. Sylvia asked what they were up to with such authority that they immediately produced a number of small grey pellets. Mrs. Gould inquired what they were.

"Bread pills," said Tony. "We were making bread pills out of bread, Mrs. Gould, to see whose was the dirtiest. Mine are much dirtier than Dora's."

"They would be," said Dr. Ford. "Horrid little pigs, both of you."

"I'll take them back to school and show them to the chaps," said Tony. "Give me yours, Dora."

Tony snatched, Dora screamed, there was a scuffle, and a large jug of milk was upset into the bread and butter and flooded the table.

"Mother, mother," shrieked Tony in unmanly accents, "my trousers! If they get milk on them it will spoil the creases!"

"Well, wipe them with your handkerchief then," said his mother.

"Mother, I can't, it would spoil my handkerchief."

"Don't be an ass," said Dr. Ford, tweaking Tony's handkerchief from his breast pocket and shaking it open. Its appearance, except for the one corner that showed, was revolting.

"How can you come out with a handkerchief like that," said his mother. "Why didn't you give it to Stoker to wash?"

"Mother, I couldn't. This is the handkerchief I kept specially for my jacket pocket, mother. I have used all the corners except this one and now it's spoilt."

"I think, Knox, we had better finish our discussion at some later date," said the Vicar, looking darkly at his youngest daughter and her friend. "But you will find, if you go into the matter thoroughly, that the carving on that pillar is not later than 1350."

"My dear Vicar," said George Knox, "only my respect for your cloth, though why one should respect cloth is a matter for discussion, the more especially as the lower orders of the clergy—no offense to you, Gould—are unfortunately prone to wear black alpaca in the summer, a material to which, made as it is from the wool of the lascivious mountain goat—the coarseness of the expression, Gould, is the bard's, not mine—no deference could possibly be paid; only this traditional respect, I say, prevents me from saying exactly what I think of you. Anyone but an obstinate, ignorant, ritualistic old maid, by which I intend no reflections on your form of worship, Vicar, for to me all forms of religion are alike, only I do wish, heartily wish, that if you must put the choir boys into frills, you would have them ironed more frequently, their appearance, I allude to the boys, being more like Toby in some wandering Punch and Judy show—and why Toby, who always used to be a fox terrier in my youth is now as often as not a brown mongrel, I cannot tell—than is consistent with true reverence; anyone else would see at a glance that the carving is at least a hundred years earlier than the arbitrary date given by you, and is indeed probably the work of the same unknown artist who was responsible for the carving in the chapter house at Barchester. Ask my old friend, the Dean of Barchester, who by the way, Laura, expressed to me the other day his profound annoyance that his verger should have been guilty of the gross discourtesy that you and I suffered at his hands, though as a matter of fact the whole affair was the fault of that friend of Tony's, that fidus Achates with his devilish mouth organ; ask anyone, I say, and see what answer you will get."

"Why not ask Lord Stoke?" said Dr. Ford.

"I will, Ford, I will. Stoke," shouted George Knox at his lordship, who was vastly enjoying a slightly flirtatious conversation with Laura and Anne at once, "what is, in your opinion, for I do not ask for a dogmatic utterance, the probable date of that carving of St. Michael and the dragon at Rising Castle?"

"Eh?" said Lord Stoke.

The Vicar, determined to get fair play, repeated the question himself.

"Oh, yes," said Lord Stoke, "nice bit of work that. I did it myself when I was a boy. Had a turn for that sort of thing, you know, and the old mason who did the repairs used to let me play about with his tools. It was meant for the old governor and his dog. I showed it to the Dean of Barchester the other day, and he thought I had quite caught the spirit of the thing."

After this Mrs. Gould said she thought she must take the children home now, as Rose wasn't supposed to be out after dark since she had pneumonia.

"Let me run you home, Mrs. Gould," said Dr. Ford. "If the Vicar and Ruth and Dora don't mind the dicky seat, we can all pack in."

Mrs. Gould gratefully accepted for herself and Rose, the Vicar stayed on all unwanted to talk to George Knox and Lord Stoke, while Sylvia said she and Dora would walk home with the Morlands.

"That isn't in the least what I meant," said Dr. Ford savagely to Sylvia, "and well you know it."

"Why?" said Sylvia.

"That you know as well as I do," said Dr. Ford, tying himself angrily into his muffler. "But I'll be even with you yet."

After goodbyes had been said, and Tony was the richer by seventeen shillings and sixpence, the walking party started for home. Dora and Tony walked in front, discussing the best way for him to spend his tips.

"I shall buy a mouth organ like Donk's," said Tony, "and have a band. I should make a jolly good band."

"They won't let you have a band at school," said Dora.

"Oh, won't they. Well, you should see my band in Morland. I have about a hundred people to play in it, and they can play absolutely every tune in the whole world."

"My Dorland band is about two hundred people," said Dora, "and they can play a lot of tunes that your band haven't even heard of yet."

"That's because they are such rotten tunes that my band simply wouldn't play them," said Tony. "By the way," he added carelessly, "there's a jolly good band at Rosebush; much better than yours."

"There isn't," shrieked Dora, hurling herself on Tony; "Rosebush hasn't got a band at all."

"Well, Dorland has only got a German band with Hitler for a conductor," said Tony, giving Dora a hearty shove. But just as they were preparing for a death grapple Sylvia came between them, took a hand of each, and ignominiously led them along, while she went on talking to Laura in a calm cheerful voice. Tony found his pulling and struggling of no avail against Sylvia's practiced grip, and resigned himself to sullen loitering from which he was jerked unsympathetically forward by Sylvia till he found it better to walk at her pace. At the Vicarage corner Dr. Ford was waiting.

"I'll see you home," he said to Sylvia. "Goodnight, Mrs. Morland. Goodnight and good luck, Tony. Here's something to buy sweets with."

Putting his arm through Sylvia's and taking Dora by the hand, he walked them away as ruthlessly as Sylvia had walked her sister and Tony.

"Look here, Sylvia," he said as soon as they were out of earshot of the Morlands, "Mrs. Mallow gets her old age pension this year and wants to go and live with her nephew the stationmaster. Then where shall I be?"

"My new job is terminated by a quarter's notice on either side," said Sylvia, "but I don't think they want to get rid of me so soon."

"Would you consider getting rid of them?"

"Why?"

"Just out of kindness, I suppose." And he put his arm around her shoulders and walked her home. As Sylvia was capable of tackling any man single-handed, it may be taken that she did not mind.

Next day, by superhuman exertions, Tony's packing was finished, the key of his trunk had been discovered in the tender of the Windsor Castle and his health certificate in the pages of "The Howling Horror," where Laura had doubtless put it herself. He and Laura were just about to start for school, when a car appeared and disgorged Dr. Ford, Sylvia, Rose and Dora.

"Sylvia and I have come to say goodbye to Tony, Mrs. Morland," said Dr. Ford, with one of his rare and difficult smiles.

He spoke with such meaning that Laura stopped the engine.

"Do you mean Sylvia and you?" she asked.

"Course he does," said Stoker, who had been standing on the doorstep with her arms rolled in her apron. "What did I say about Mrs. Mallow getting her old age pension? Miss Sylvia's a bit young, but she's got an old head on young shoulders, as the saying goes, and the doctor isn't getting any younger, so I dare say it was all meant. Don't you let your poor mother's cook, as she calls herself, make the cake, Miss Sylvia. You don't want to be starting your honeymoon with the indigestion. I'll make you one."

"Thank you, Stoker," said the unperturbed Sylvia.

"My dears, I haven't time to stay to understand," said Laura. "I've got to take Tony back to school. Don't do anything rash till I come back. Both come in after dinner and tell me all about it. Stoker seems to understand it all much better than I do, but I am so distracted today."

Rose and Dora were eagerly talking to Tony as he sat in the car. He had draped himself in the languid manner he considered suitable to trousers and his round face looked incredibly small under his new bowler, while his ears looked incredibly large.

"It's not really true about the Rosebush band, is it, Tony?" asked Dora anxiously.

"Oh, Tony, do I really have a band at Rosebush?" said Rose at the same moment.

"The whole thing is just imagination," said Tony.

As his mother started the car again he raised his hat courteously to the little girls, replaced it carefully on his well-brilliantined hair, and sinking back with a worldly air into his seat remarked to his mother:

"Those kids actually believe in Dorland and Morland, mother. But, of course, they're only kids."

COLOPHON

This book is being reissued as part of Moyer Bell's Angela Thirkell Series. If you are interested and want more information contact the Angela Thirkell Society, P.O. Box 7798, San Diego, CA 92167 or email JOINATS@aol.com

The text of this book was seet in Caslon, a type-face designed by William Caslon I (1692-1766). This face designed in 1725 has gone through many incarnations. It was the mainstay of British printers for over one hundred years and remains very popular today. The version used here is Adobe Caslon. The display faces are Nicholas Jenson Open, Calligraphic 421, and Adobe Caslon.

This book was typeset by Rhode Island Book Composition, Kingston, Rhode Island and printed by Versa Press, East Peroria, Illinois on acid free paper.